UNDER THE BROKEN SKY

MARIKO NAGAI

UNDER THE BROKEN SKY

Christy Ottaviano Books
Henry Holt and Company
New York

Henry Holt and Company, *Publishers since 1866*
Henry Holt® is a registered trademark of Macmillan Publishing Group, LLC
120 Broadway, New York, NY 10271
mackids.com

Library of Congress Cataloging-in-Publication Data

Names: Nagai, Mariko, author.
Title: Under the broken sky / Mariko Nagai.
Description: First edition. | New York : Henry Holt and Company, 2019. | "Christy
  Ottaviano Books." | Summary: When Soviet troops invade Japanese-occupied Manchuria
  during the last days of World War II, twelve-year-old Natsu Kimura must care for her
  younger sister as they struggle to survive and return to Japan.
Identifiers: LCCN 2018021063 | ISBN 978-1-250-15921-2 (hardcover)
Subjects: LCSH: World War, 1939–1945—China—Manchuria—Juvenile fiction. |
  Manchuria (China)—History—1931–1945—Juvenile fiction. | CYAC: Novels in verse. |
  World War, 1939–1945—China—Manchuria—Fiction. | Manchuria (China)—
  History—1931–1945—Fiction. | Survival—Fiction. | Refugees—Fiction. |
  Sisters—Fiction.
Classification: LCC PZ7.5.N34 Un 2019 | DDC [Fic]—dc23
LC record available at https://lccn.loc.gov/2018021063

Our books may be purchased in bulk for promotional, educational, or business use. Please
contact your local bookseller or the Macmillan Corporate and Premium Sales Department
at (800) 221-7945 ext. 5442 or by email at MacmillanSpecialMarkets@macmillan.com.

First edition, 2019
Printed in the United States of America by LSC Communications,
Harrisonburg, Virginia

1 3 5 7 9 10 8 6 4 2

For Deborah,
who believed in this more than I did
—M.N.

UNDER THE BROKEN SKY

PART ONE

SUMMER

A Manchurian Birthday

Horse presses herself against me,
and I press my hand against her neck,
excitement running through us

like the summer wind.
"Remember not to go too far.
Ride close to the Wall.

I'll keep my eye on you
from the gate," Tochan says
and raises the rifle to his chest;

Asa glares at me
next to him, still angry that I get
to ride Horse instead of her.

We take off, fast and then gallop
even faster, and soon enough,
the Wall becomes a dot behind us.

My braids bang against my back,
as if they are urging me
to go faster, faster, farther away.

Way too soon, Horse slows
down to a canter, and then stops altogether
as if she remembers Tochan's warning.

"A bit more," I urge her,
"a little farther."
Just a bit more so I can go

to where the sky meets the earth,
where the sun explodes
into brilliant colors before it hides

to let the night take its place.
Horse's heart beats in the same rhythm
as my heart, our hearts beat

together. Her steps are my own steps.
She is me and I am her.
It's my birthday. I am twelve.

TOCHAN'S WARNING

Horse keeps walking slowly
but suddenly she stops
and cranes her neck back,

her eyes peering into mine.
"Yes, I know," I pat her neck.
It's as if she knows that we have

gone far enough. Tochan says
that outside the Wall,
anything can happen:

the sudden cold can make you
lose feeling and make you fall
asleep, never to wake up.

He says that outside the Wall,
there are Chinese, Russians,
bad men all. One of the first

things he did when Kachan
—my mother—died,
even before we were done missing her

was to show me where he hides
his gun. "Just in case," he said as he pulled
it out, along with a hand grenade,

from under his pillow.
This is how you load the gun.
This is how you pull the trigger.

This is how you pull the pin out
of the grenade, but count one-two-
three before you throw it.

And he told me that before the Japanese
moved into Manchuria, this land used to
belong to the Chinese, and that they are still

angry after all these years. That's why
there's the Wall, two meters thick
and high as the sky around the settlement.

That's why when we walk to school,
I have to go with Asa
and come back in a group.

That's why we have to carry rifles
when we go to the neighboring settlement.
That's why the gate closes after the curfew.

That's why I can never ride Horse out
to the plain without asking Tochan first.
Horse neighs. The sky is still

light—it's summer and the sun won't set
until ten—but we need to go home.
I turn Horse around, and she seems happy

that we are returning, away
from this dangerous big prairie
where anything can happen.

Wind blows, carrying with it
a hint of the cold night to come,
and with it an imaginary baying of a wolf.

GOING TOO FAR

The sky is still lit white,
though half the sky is deep blue,

deep purple-black—the color
of the water when you grind

the ink against the stone
for calligraphy, the colors swirling

then darkening with each grind—
when Horse and I head back.

I pass by a Manchu's broken-
down hut, and a pig snorts loudly,

and the house spits out angry
smoke. I click my tongue

to let Horse know we need
to move faster.

She goes into a slow canter.
And the Wall the size of a dot

becomes bigger and bigger,
and I see someone standing there.

It's Tochan waiting with a rifle,
his anger crackling like firecrackers

at New Year's. I flinch
as if he's just slapped me,

and Horse shudders hard
as if she can feel my fear.

TOCHAN'S ANGER

From the way he is standing—
his back straight and his legs apart—
I can tell it's the stance he gets

when he is worried-angry,
just like he was when Kachan's
water broke too early and she was howling

from so much pain. Then Tochan stood
with his legs apart, as well—
this time by the doorway

to our hut, angry-worried. Angry
at the world, angry at the baby
for being stubborn, and even more worried

at Kachan, especially when she started to give up,
breathing slower and slower,
until Asa came sliding out slower still.

Auntie told me to catch the baby,
and I held wet, sticky Asa in my arms,
while Kachan closed her eyes and stopped

breathing and Asa wailed loud.
Tochan stood by the doorway,
not letting Kachan's soul out of the house.

He stood there, with his legs apart,
trying to hold on to her, trying to make her
stay, but she left and he got angry-sad.

Then he got angry-worried about me and Asa, just like he's worried-angry about me right now.

BROKEN PROMISES

"You promised," Tochan starts,
"you promised you wouldn't go
beyond the hill where I couldn't see you."

Tochan raises his arm
and I flinch and Horse flinches,
but instead, he puts his hand

under my elbow and gently
pulls me down from Horse
the way he touches Asa's cheek,

the way he roughens my hair,
the way he talks to chickens and Horse,
gently, in a hushed tone,

and I know he's not worried-angry anymore.
We pass by Auntie's house, pass
the communal well and the latrines,

pass the bathhouse and our chicken coop,
to our home where I see Asa's face peering out
from the lit window, her eyes laughing

and her mouth moving, *You're in real trouble.*
I stick my tongue out; Asa laughs.
Tochan doesn't look at me.

He doesn't say a word.
He keeps walking fast
as if I am a ghost he doesn't see.

"I'm sorry," I whisper,
and Tochan turns around.
"I'm just relieved that

you are safely home. I'm just happy,
especially since this is your birthday, Natsu,"
and everything is all right between us.

The Best Birthday Present

Asa bursts out
of the front door
like a colt bolting out

from the stable,
"Are you in trouble?"
she chants, "Are you in trouble?"

Tochan grabs her
and lifts her onto
his shoulder,

"It's Natsu's birthday,
of course she's not
in trouble," and he laughs.

"Happy birthday, my little summer,"
he says softly, just like
Kachan used to call me,

my little summer. Asa laughs
from her high perch on Tochan's
shoulder, and pulls out a piece

of paper from her pocket.
There I am: on Horse
dashing through the golden prairie.

"Happy birthday, Natsu-chan,"
Asa chants, "happy birthday,
my big big sister!"

LETTERS TO THE SOLDIERS

Tochan sits on the mat woven
from corn husk, cleaning the blade
of the hoe for work in the fields tomorrow,

and Asa sits next to him,
drawing pictures on the months-old
newspapers. I sit at the table

and write letters to the soldiers
fighting for Japan on the islands
in the Pacific so I can put them

in the comfort packages
we'll be packing at school.
I lick the lead

of the pencil,
and I start
in my best handwriting,

Thank you for fighting for the Emperor,
for Japan, and for all of us "behind the guns"
at home. Don't worry about us.

We will fight to the last man and woman
if the American devils come,
so please kill as many Americans as possible

and please die honorably like a soldier
of the Japanese Imperial Army and Navy.
Just like I was taught at school,

our teachers telling us this is the only
kind of letter fit for our fighting soldiers.
I fold the letter in fourths, put one

of Asa's drawings inside, seal them
into an envelope, and start on the next.
All around our cottage,

the darkness has yet to arrive,
the sun lingering in the horizon
like a lazy cow in July.

But inside, the temperature drops
and darkness is creeping one inch
at a time along the wall.

KACHAN'S GHOST

Some nights like tonight when I can't sleep,
I count memories of Kachan like people count
sheep. I remember her singing:

she only sang one song about a girl who went
to America wearing red shoes. I remember
when she used to sit really close by the lamp

to sew or mend, she would always lick the end
of the thread, squinting her eyes, before she put it through
the eye of the needle. It made Tochan laugh every time.

Laughing is something that Tochan doesn't do now.
He must have buried his laughter inside
Kachan's coffin with her body. I remember Tochan yelling

at me to keep the water boiling so he could melt
the frozen ground. Only then could he bury Kachan.
I remember Goat living in our hut

that long winter so we could give milk to Asa.
And when Goat died, we were all sad
but thanked her for a good dinner that night.

I remember before Asa came, Tochan,
Kachan, and I slept in the shape of the Chinese
character for *river*, three parallel lines, with me in the middle.

And when Asa came, I slept where Kachan once slept,
with Asa in the middle. Tochan calls my mom
Kachan—mother—and that's why I call her this.

I also know that every morning,
Tochan talks to Kachan at the altar,
asking her to look after Asa and me.

That makes me real sad, though I don't tell
Tochan I hear what he says. Sometimes, I know why
Kachan died: because I didn't love her enough.

If I had loved her enough, she would've wanted
to stay with us. And sometimes,
I remember that feeling right after she died,

the feeling of my heart breaking
into pieces like an icicle
shattering against the ground in early spring,

and I never want to feel like that, ever again.
That's why I don't like to remember Kachan that much—
All I remember is sadness.

On the Way to School

"Horse, see you later,"
Asa yells, as we run
out of the house

past the well, and past
Auntie's hens,
"Natsu and Asa,

are you late again?"
Auntie yells, making
the hens flap their wings,

as if they're keeping time
with her voice, and even
they are chiding us.

We run toward the Wall,
"Natsu-chan, you are
too fast," Asa whines.

So I slow down
to let her catch up.
"Oh look,"

Asa points to the sky,
"that cloud looks
like a camel."

"You don't know what
a camel looks like,"
I tell her, keeping

my ear alert to the bell.
"I do, too, and I want
to be a camel when I grow up."

I roll my eyes. "You wanted
to be a goat, too, before Goat died
so you could talk to her.

Before that, you wanted to be a hen.
Then a wolf. A bird before that."
The bell starts ringing;

school's about to begin. "We need
to run now," I yell, running even faster,
and I hear Asa behind me: "Don't leave

me, I can't keep up!" One. Two.
Three. The bell will stop soon
and we'll have to clean

the bathroom for the next seven
days if we're late again.
I run. And run. I hear Asa behind me,

and we both run away from the Wall.
We run through the wheat field,
we run through the blue sky.

At School

Put the rolled-up bandages,
a total of three, in the bottom of the hemp bag.

Place a packet of cigarettes, the ones
with a golden chrysanthemum insignia

on the right side atop the bandages;
put the box of sweet caramels

in a yellow box in the opposite
corner, and put the *senninbari*—

a good-luck charm of one thousand
red stitches of embroidered tiger—

between the candy and the cigarettes.
A tube of toothpaste. A shaving razor.

Slide the magazine, any magazine,
into the bag. Don't forget the letters.

I tie the neck of the bag.
I start on another one.

All around me, hands blur,
almost like fast-flapping wings of chickens,

all moving quickly to finish the quota
for our brave soldiers.

WE ARE THE EMPEROR'S CHILDREN

We stand at attention
with bamboo spears in our hands.

Vice Principal yells,
Stab the American devil!

And I thrust the bamboo
spear to the left.

Kill the enemy!
And I thrust the spear

to the right,
the imaginary enemy

in the shape of a straw
scarecrow. We move

as one with the call:
Kill the American devil!

We thrust the spears
as one: *Take down as many*

enemies as you can!
Kill as many enemies

as you can when you die!
We are the Emperor's children.

We are the children
of the Sun Goddess.

We are the citizens
of the Rising Sun.

We are from the country
where the wind from the gods

blows in times of need to bring us victory.
We will die for the Emperor,

just like those special forces pilots
who smash their planes against the American

ships in the South Sea.
We will die for the Emperor

just like those brave soldiers
who make their last charge

to protect His Majesty the Emperor.
Stab the American devil!

And I thrust the bamboo
spear to the left.

Get ready to kill the enemy!
We throw down the spears

and grab the dried corncobs.
One, two, three, throw the grenades.

Yellow jagged cobs hit the vice
principal. *No, no, not me!*

I try to hold my laughter
but it flies out like impatient Horse.

WATERMELON THIEF

Asa and I walk home from school—
the fields on both sides of us
bulging with an almost

ready harvest of watermelons
and potatoes, cabbages and tomatoes.
We walk through fields of lettuce—

wheat heavy with husks,
and that's when we see him:
a Manchu boy in rags holding

a watermelon as big
as his own head.
I yell, *Thief, thief!*

I start toward him
with my bamboo spear raised high
just like I was taught,

and he takes off like a rabbit
with the watermelon held
above his head,

a boy dirty and small,
not much older than Asa.
"Natsu-chan, he's taking our watermelon!"

Asa yells loudly.
I whack him with the spear
and he falls, still holding

on to the watermelon,
and he screams, *"Riben Guizi,"*
Japanese devil!

I kick him. Asa screams even louder,
"Natsu-chan, kick him." Then,
"Don't hurt him!" and he sputters,

"Japan's going to lose
and when they do, I'll kill you!"
He lies like a Chinese, and I kick

him for it. I kick him again and
again and Asa kicks him, too

but as quick as a rabbit,
he jumps up, still holding the watermelon
to his chest, and scampers away.

I run after him but he's gone,
somewhere in the field.
"I hope we didn't hurt him

too much," Asa says,
as she kicks a rock,
but my face still burns

like the chimney in wintertime,
my heart beating fast: he's a liar
he's a liar, but his words,

Japan's going to lose
are ringing in my head,
swirling and buzzing

like big fat mosquitoes that keep
whining in the middle of the night,
and they just won't go away.

WALK OF DEFEAT

White hens peck
the invisible worms
and seem to laugh

at me as we walk
by Auntie's house.
I kick them

and they fly away
in surprise.
"You no good girl!"

I hear Auntie's voice
ringing out from her hut.
"I know it's you, Natsu Kimura!

I'm going to tell
your pa!" And I stick
my tongue out at her.

Asa sticks her tongue
out as well; then pulls it back
quickly, "Don't. Auntie'll tell

Tochan, and then, we'll be
in real trouble." But I already feel
a little better, not too much,

but good enough
to feel that I beat Auntie's
hens into submission.

THE SEA OF GOLD

I straighten my back.
The wheat is almost ready.

Two more days,
and we will be busy

with the harvest.
Tochan seems miles

and miles away,
his back bent—

the only thing I can see
is his straw hat

moving up and down
above the sea of gold—

and Asa at the edge
of the field, chasing after

birds that are trying
to land on this golden ocean.

I move my arms left,
right, parting the waves

of gold, I swim
through the sea of gold,

I swim closer and closer
to Tochan and Asa.

Lies Told Late at Night

I lick the tip of the pencil again,
about to start another letter,
when I feel Tochan watching me.

The shadow from the lamp is making
his chin waver but his eyes are steady.
He says, "You look like your mother

when you do that. She loved to write
letters, and she would always lick
the tip of the pencil, just like you do, before

she began. Do you remember?"
And I nod, though I can't tell him
that I don't remember Kachan that much.

Moments are what I have—
how she would tell me stories,
how she would stand by the well

to crank the handle to bring up the bucket—
but the only face of Kachan I remember
is the photo on the altar, where she is smiling,

and she's never moving in my memory,
like everything I remember
about her is a series of photos.

Six years is a long time to be gone:
Kachan's been gone half of my life,
and all of Asa's life.

I lie to Tochan so that he doesn't get sad,
I lie to Tochan because I know he misses her,
I lie to Tochan so I can will myself to remember.

A MESSENGER IN THE NIGHT

The knock on the door
came late at night.
The knock came

as we were already
asleep atop *ondol*,
the heated floor

in the shape of the Chinese
character for river—
three parallel strokes:

Tochan to the left,
Asa in the middle,
and me to the right.

After the knock came,
Tochan got out of the bedding
with a gun in his hand,

and when he opened the door,
the settlement secretary
stood there, the hint

of autumn wind swirling
into the house,
making me shiver.

"Congratulations,
you have been called
by His Majesty our Emperor

to serve the Empire," he said,
but he did not smile.
His hand shook as he pulled

out the *akagami*, the draft
notice. "You are to report
to the settlement office the day after

tomorrow with all your weapons,
food, and your horse,"
he said, looking down.

Tochan just stood there.
My heart beat so loudly.
After thousands and hundreds

of heartbeats, Tochan bowed
deeply. "Thank you
for the good news. I'm honored

to serve His Majesty the Emperor
and our glorious Empire of Japan,"
and he saluted smartly,

the way he used to when he was
joking, just like he said he had
to do when he was drafted

a long time ago when there was
no war. He said he hated
the army except that he was never hungry

like he was at home.
Only this time he wasn't joking.
This time it was serious.

I should've been happy
that Tochan was called to serve.
But why is it that even after

so many hours, even after Tochan
and I went back to bed, that I can't sleep?
I feel something heavy

on my chest, like someone is
stepping on it and I can't breathe.
But I know I'm not the only one:

I hear Tochan moving, tossing
and turning. Asa lies there
with her mouth slightly open.

Promises to Tochan

Tochan calls Asa and me
to sit in front of him.
"This is very important," he says,

and opens the old military backpack.
He takes things out one by one:
the family registry form,

birth certificates,
deeds to the house and land,
passports for three,

dried umbilical cords, family seals,
the black lacquered tablet
with Kachan's otherworldly

name beautifully written in gold ink,
Kachan's ring and small gold
fillings he had kept after she died,

postal saving books, family photos.
Then he pulls out the handgun
from under the pillow and puts that

in the bag. "Repeat after me,"
he says, and makes us repeat
the address of his family in Japan.

"Remember this," he says.
"If anything happens, grab
the bag and run as fast

as you can and find Auntie.
There's a chance that our settlement
may be attacked."

"By whom?" Asa asks.
Tochan looks at Asa, then me,
like he's trying to figure out

how to say things he doesn't know
how to answer. Then, "It may
be the Chinese. It may be

the Soviets. It may be the Americans.
Go to Auntie's. She will take you two back
to Japan if something happens."

He pauses and looks straight into my eyes.
"And if there's no one left,
you need to stay together and go

back to Japan on your own.
You know how to use the gun
but use it only when you have to, Natsu.

Asa, you have to
listen to your big sister,
you two have to stick together,

no matter what." He stares
at us, making us submit to his order.
We stare back. I nod. I understand.

Tigers Travel One Thousand Li and Back

With a red thread and a needle,
I sew a stitch, then tie a knot
on the back. I'm not sure who

Tochan will be fighting.
I sew another stitch.
Not the Soviets; they've signed

the treaty with His Majesty
the Emperor, promising not to fight.
Each stitch follows

the outline of a tiger
I drew on a cotton fabric.
Not the Manchurians—

why would Tochan fight
them when we've been
their friends ever since

Manchuria was created
fourteen years ago,
five races as one.

Senninbari—needles
of a thousand people—
a good-luck charm every

soldier is supposed to keep.
Not the Americans;
they aren't here yet.

Tigers can travel one thousand *li*
and back, they always come back.
Like Tochan, who will travel

one thousand *li* and come back.
So who is Tochan
supposed to fight?

The Night Pushed Away

The room is slowly turning white.
The night is slowly being pushed

back to where it came from.
Auntie's cock crows once,

then twice, singing of the morning
just around the corner.

Asa is curled up and Tochan lies
with his arm around her.

I make my last stitch
and the tiger moves in the light.

My Mind Like the Running Horse

My mind doesn't stay still.
I can't sit still.
The sun rose all too

early, and I hear
Tochan get out of bed
like any other morning,

and Asa sucks on her thumb
and Tochan tries to pull it out,
but Asa keeps pushing it back in

and he smiles and lets her be,
just like any other morning,
like all the mornings in the world.

Tochan raises his eyebrows,
like he's asking me a question,
"Did you sleep at all?"

I rub my tired eyes. I want
this morning to last
as long as it can.

A Prayer Rice

I put the freshly cooked
rice, burning hot,
in my hand

and make it into a ball
the size of the biggest
potato with both hands,

pressing, saying a prayer
with each press:
Tochan, stay safe.

Tochan, come home soon.
And a rice ball comes out of a prayer,
and I line them up

in my lunch box,
three of them just like us:
Tochan, Asa, and me.

THE ELDEST SON

I take tea out to the barn
like Tochan does
every morning.

But this morning
he's getting Horse ready
for a journey. The air at this hour

carries a hint of fall
still a distance away
but crawling closer

like the last chime of the school
bell when you are late.
He turns around

and smiles and takes
the cup from my hand.
I put my hand on Horse

as she nuzzles her cheek
against my head.
"Tochan, take care of her,"

I tell him, and he laughs,
"She'll probably take care of me."
He turns away and takes a brush

to Horse's back. Heartbeats
translate into seconds,
into minutes passing,

and the time only goes forward.
Suddenly, he says,
"You can ride Horse like a boy

and you can farm like one, too.
You're like the boy I never had.
Now that I have to leave,

you are the *chonan*—the eldest son."
Something stings my nose,
and I look away so that he won't see

my eyes welling up,
"I need you to be strong.
I need you to be brave.

No matter what."
All I can say,
so that the tears won't fall,

is "Tochan, fight well,"
and I hand him the *senninbari*,
my stitches uneven and big.

His face seems to crack,
like the glass window during the coldest
winter nights, and he says,

"You're old enough
to understand when I tell you
that I may not come back.

Be strong, Natsu.
You're the only one
who can look after Asa.

You're the only one who can take
her back to Japan."
And he pulls me close to him

and holds me tight.
He smells of the late-summer prairie
and the Manchurian soil

and cabbages and earth
and sleep he didn't have.
"I promise I will come find you,

no matter where you are
in the world, I will find you two,"
he whispers, "I'll come back alive."

Horse stomps her hoof.
I bury my face in Tochan's chest
to stop the time from moving forward.

MR. SOLDIER, MY TOCHAN

We walk toward
the school, Asa riding,
Tochan leading Horse

while I walk next to him.
"Be good," Tochan tells Asa.
"You must listen to Natsu-chan,

because Tochan has to go to war."
And Asa claps her hands
and then salutes,

"Mr. Soldier!"
Tochan laughs and salutes.
The sky seems to widen

with his laughter
and I wish this walk
will never ever end.

WHAT TOCHAN TAKES WITH HIM TO THE WAR

Three rice balls in my aluminum lunch box;
a *senninbari* I had made for good luck and for speedy homecoming;
a photo of me and Asa;

a bag of carrots for Horse;
Asa's drawing: Tochan, Asa, and me sleeping in the shape of the river;
a little pouch with a strand of Kachan's hair;

a rifle and all the ammunitions;
a water canteen;
a rucksack with his fur coat rolled up inside;

Horse;
a photo of Kachan;
my prayer and love.

Long Live the Emperor

The schoolyard is filled
with all the neighbors.
There's Masa-chan and her father,

short and bundled up in a fur coat
though it's sweltering hot.
There's Kazuo's father,

tall, his bald head glistening
with sweat. There's Yoshiko's brother
who can carry a colt on his back

and walk to the next settlement and back he's so strong.
There's Taro, Auntie's son, and Auntie scolding
him as she always does, and as always, he is smiling

like he's not really hearing a thing.
There are fathers and brothers
standing, milling about with their rifles and horses.

There's Toshio passing out
Japanese flags he drew on papers.
There's the settlement leader with a clipboard,

counting heads and calling out names.
I stand close to Tochan and hold his hand,
big, warm, and hard like Horse's hooves.

Everyone is saying good-bye.
Everyone is saying, *Fight well for the country.*
Everyone is saying, *Long live the Emperor.*

I'm supposed to say, like my teachers taught me,
Be brave and kill as many enemies as you can,
but these words don't sound true,

though I've written them dozens
and hundreds of times to soldiers I don't know.
And before I know it, "Be safe,"

rolls out of my mouth
and these words feel just right.
"Tochan, come back soon," Asa says,

and Tochan smiles his sad smile
and a voice calls out,
"Get ready, we're leaving."

Tochan hugs Asa, hugs me,
and whispers into my ear,
"Remember our promise,"

and I nod. He gathers Asa and me into
a big circle of hug and Horse neighs.
The men and boys all get up,

but I'm not ready. "Horse, take care of Tochan," I yell.
I put my hand on her neck,
and she nuzzles against my cheek.

Men and boys stand in line
and they leave as one.
We stand there until they are a big dot

in the field and too soon, they disappear
behind the curve of the horizon.
Asa and I hold hands and walk

home, where I know there is no Tochan.
There is no Horse. But we can pretend
otherwise. Just a little longer.

EVERYTHING IS THE SAME, NOTHING IS THE SAME

The settlement is exactly the same,
the walls still thick and the well still stands.
Chickens still cluck and peck around about the yard.

Yet the stable stands empty;
the horses are gone. Behind me,
women and girls enter into

their quiet houses. No man is around.
This is a ghost town, though I've only seen
it in a movie. Asa and I enter our house,

suddenly so empty, though it smells
of Tochan if I close
my eyes and sniff long enough.

That's when I hear it:
"I'm going to live here with you two
now that my son and your pa are drafted."

Auntie enters our hut like an autumn gale.
My stomach sinks. Asa wrinkles her face.
Tochan didn't say anything about that.

He said that I was supposed
to take care of Asa but said nothing
about Auntie coming to live with us.

"Did you know?" Asa asks and I shake my head.
"From today on"—she drops her bundle—
"we are living as a family.

"Your pa said to look after you two."
And I know that Tochan probably did.
He also knows how much I hate this enemy.

AUNTIE, THE ENEMY OF MY TWELFTH YEAR

Auntie clucks her tongue
at us as she would to her chickens,
scolding that my hands are too dirty,

that Asa's too skinny and she needs
to eat more, that my pickles are too salty,
and that Asa's too quiet. Auntie came

to our house like the yellow wind
that comes every spring, unwanted,
causing itches and aches in our eyes

and even under our clothes.
She makes me itch like I'm carrying a flea.
She came with a big bag full of her stuff

and leaves everything everywhere,
the house becoming hers.
She even brought her hens with her

and they boss our chickens around
like she bosses us. She came in
and rearranged our chairs,

our table, pots, and pans,
cleaning away Tochan's touches
until he's almost gone.

Asa tells me not to,
but I stand firm, my legs apart
and my arms to my sides,

and tell her to leave it,
leave everything as it is.
Before I can stop myself,

I'm shouting, "This ain't your home.
We're just letting you stay here.
But as soon as Japan wins the war,

as soon as Tochan and Taro come back,
you'll have to go back home where you belong!"
She clucks her tongue, just like she always does

when she doesn't like something, and tells me
that it might be a long while
before they can come home.

Says she can't read newspapers
but she can see what's going on,
and what's going on isn't good.

"You girls training with spears;
drafting men in settlements
right before the harvest season.

Things are going bad,
I know it just like I know when
it's going to rain real bad,"

she says, and clucks her tongue again,
and I tell her that she's unpatriotic.
I tell her that Japan will never lose,

but as I'm saying this,
I hear that Chinese boy's voice
ringing in my head.

I see Tochan's sad face
when he told me he might not come back,
and I shake my head to shake off

the voice. She looks and looks at me
until I think she's trying to stare me into
submission like Tochan used to with Horse.

"My son is a good boy, but he's real slow.
Your father's served before, and he's too old,
but they were both taken away anyway," she says.

She's lying. She's a liar
and I hate her. I take Asa's hand
and run outside, slamming

the door so Auntie'd go deaf.
Asa tugs my hand.
"Is she angry with us?"

I tell her she's our new enemy,
she's like Churchill and that new
American devil president, Truman.

I tell her we're running away.
We should follow Tochan,
but she shakes her head.

"I like Auntie's cooking better than yours,"
and with that, Asa runs back inside.
A traitor! I run to the barn

only to remember Horse went
with Tochan. So I kick the beam
where Horse used to rub her belly

when she itched but kicking it
only hurts my toes. I kick the pile
of hay, and anger mushrooms

like bluebottles in summer.
Auntie is the enemy of my twelfth year:
she is Churchill, Roosevelt,

Stalin, the evil enemy
all combined, here to stay
with the army of chickens.

SCHOOL

When we get to school,
we are supposed to bow
to the shrine by the gate

where the Emperor's portrait
is hidden behind the closed
doors. We line up,

divided by grades,
and salute to the east,
where the Emperor is.

Then we recite our pledge
to the Emperor
and to the Great Empire of Japan.

But today, no one seems
to want to, like we usually do.
Instead of defense drills with spears,

a substitute teacher
reads to us from a book
of folktales, about a thumb-size

boy and all of these
stories we used to hear
but haven't ever since we had

to practice with spears.
For one hour, I forgot about Tochan,
I forgot about Mr. Suzuki, my teacher.

And about the war we are not
supposed to forget but I did,
just for an hour.

THE ENEMY IS CRUEL

Banging of pots starts
before the sunrise.
Banging of doors starts

as the sun comes through the window.
Auntie moves around
the room as if she is the yellow

sand-wind that comes
every spring,
leaving sand everywhere,

and she yells
that we need to get
up. Asa lies

in the futon like a big round
ball, pretending she doesn't
hear, and I don't move, either,

curled up and playing deaf.
Auntie comes in
and pulls the futon

from under us
and we roll out
like two balls,

rolling on the cold
floor. She tells me
to go feed the chickens

and gather the eggs
and if I don't, then no
breakfast for me.

I try to make
Asa go for me,
but she runs out to get

the bucket so she can go
get water from the well.
I go to the chickens

and kick them
but even they laugh at me,
pecking noisily.

Nothing is the same
without Tochan and Horse.
I miss Tochan so much.

HANGING HEADS

Wheat heads hang their heads heavily,
stalks bending from the weight.
This is the settlement with no men.

Only old men and women and children.
The Matsuhashis' watermelons lie overripe.
The Kojimas' potato leaves are browning.

Auntie just shakes her head:
"So much wasted. That's what war
does, so many things change."

With only Asa and me, we can't harvest on our own.
My wheat seems to be angry at me.
But our field isn't the only one.

SUNDAY

Asa and I walk
hand in hand
through the garden

behind our house, her hand
small and warm
like a freshly laid egg.

"Natsu-chan," she says
suddenly, stopping,
then points at the sky.

A bird. Then another.
And another. A geese
migration. Fall is almost

here. And once fall is done,
it's winter. When Kachan died.
I push that thought away

but I shiver. "Are you cold,
Natsu-chan?" I tell her no,
but Asa puts her arms

around my middle,
and I put my arms
around her shoulders.

We become one,
just like the day she was born
and she fell into my arms

even before the umbilical cord
was cut away, and I held her
close to me because

Kachan couldn't hold her anymore,
because Kachan couldn't hold
me anymore,

and now that Tochan is away,
I am the only one
who can hold her.

A SUMMER NIGHT

Auntie bends closer
to the light to better
see the stitches.

Asa lies on her stomach
as she draws a picture
of a horse. I should

be writing
a letter to the soldiers
but I have nothing to say.

Instead, I imagine Tochan up north
with Horse. Where are they tonight,
I wonder, are they staying warm?

Here the night is quiet.
Bugs are singing
their last summer songs,

and it is all quiet
on the plain of Manchuria,
and Asa says, without looking

up, "I miss Tochan.
Tell me a story, Natsu-chan,
just like Tochan used to."

Auntie looks up from her mending.
My mind goes blank.
"Didn't know you told stories,"

Auntie snorts. Hot fire flashes
through my body, my face burns.
I glare at Auntie. I'll show her.

And I start. I tell a story
about Tochan and Horse,
and how they travel through

the golden prairie and how
they fought against thousands of
Soviets all by themselves . . .

on and on the words come rolling
out and Asa is fast asleep.
Auntie nods, "Not bad, not bad at all."

LIES I TELL ASA

Our carrots and potatoes
are almost done,
and the husks

are bowing
from the weight,
heavy for reaping.

Asa says
she doesn't like war
because it took Tochan

away, because it makes
me grumpy
and Auntie mean.

I tell her Tochan will
come home soon
though there's no weight

to what I say. I tell her
this every day. I tell myself
this every day, too,

because lies can come
true if you tell them long
enough and hard enough.

AUGUST IN MANCHURIA

The land is flat
and quiet.
The hens cluck

in their sleep
once in a while.
The night comes late

here in northern
Manchuria in August,
turning the sky white-

blue before turning
deep blue,
bringing with it a sheet

of stars so bright
even the wolves howl
in awe.

PART TWO

LATE SUMMER

Winter Coats, Leather Shoes, Tochan's Backpack

Someone is calling my name.
Someone calls my name,

from far away, or is it close . . .
"Wake . . . ," someone yells. "Natsu."

Someone calls, "Natsu,
Natsu," and more urgently,

"Up! Wake up." The voice is in my head,
the voice is out of my head,

and I wake up startled.
"The Soviets are here," Auntie yells.

"They are coming. We need to leave. Now."
She's pushing Asa into a thick coat.

She's balling up leftover rice into rice balls.
She's pulling out my thickest coat

from the closet. She's pulling my arm.
"Wake up, Natsu. We need to leave."

She moves like the wind, this way, that way,
and I don't know what's going on

but she keeps insisting, "Natsu, put
your coat on," and I don't know what's going

on, but I know what's going on
like I do in a dream.

Asa puts on her leather shoes.
Auntie hoists the backpack she carried

here over her winter coat.
I pull on the coat. I pull up Tochan's backpack

and tighten the straps to my body.
We need to leave. We need to leave

now. I don't know what's going on.
I *do* know what's going on.

I don't know what's going on.
I don't want to know what's going on.

Running

We don't lock the door.
We don't release the chickens

from the henhouse.
We don't board up the windows.

Holding Asa's hand,
I run out of the homestead,

Auntie telling us to hurry,
to hurry and follow her,

just like Tochan told me to do:
run if anything happens.

Run if anything happens.
And something is happening.

On the Way to School

We walk
fast through
the dark

dirt road
to the schoolhouse,
my hand

in Auntie's,
my other hand
holding

Asa's sweaty
hand.
The familiar

road made
unfamiliar
with darkness,

with fear,
and Asa's breath
made visible

with cold air.
We walk.
We walk fast,

our hearts pounding
as one.
We walk fast

and firm,
and the voices
from far away

come closer
and closer
as we near

the school
until we go
through the open gate

and we enter
into voices,
words broken up.

Soviets . . .
Train . . . Where is . . .
The neighboring . . .

Leave . . . Now . . .
Japanese Army . . .
The words broken

up into fragments
like someone threw
a piece of ice

against the wall,
shattering it
into millions of pieces.

Time Stops Moving

People. Luggage.   Voices.
         Sleepiness.   Fear.   Wakefulness.

It's still night and   the morning
         is   far   away in hours.

We all stand   like chickens
                          with a wolf   circling

outside the cage, chirping,   flapping
         our arms, craning   necks   left and   right,

waiting for someone   to tell   us
         that the drill   was a success, a joke,

we've all passed.   And now,   we   can
                  go home.

THE ATTACK

Principal Ohara coughs.
We become quiet.

Principal Ohara coughs.
The night stills.

He opens his mouth,
then closes it, his words lost

somewhere in his head.
Then he begins: "We received

an urgent message saying
that the Soviets have crossed

over the border and they are
heading this way.

We need to evacuate now
to Harbin." We swallow

hard as one.
No one speaks.

"Boys over thirteen will remain
and defend the settlement.

Girls over thirteen will
arm yourselves and defend

the evacuation party.
We must leave immediately."

"What about our homes?" someone yells.
"What about our crops?" another yells.

"We can come back when the Soviets
are defeated by our Imperial soldiers.

But right now, we must leave.
We can't waste any more minutes,

we need to evacuate,"
he yells over

the questions.
"We can defend our land!"

and a chorus of *Yes! Yes!* rings out,
until we remember

there are no men left.
But I feel the weight

of the gun in Tochan's bag
on my back. I can fight,

I know I can
just like I've been taught.

MORSE CODE

Auntie grips my hand harder.
"You heard the principal.

We are leaving. Don't you let
go of my hand or Asa's, you hear?"

And I nod. I grip Asa's hand harder,
and grip Auntie's hand hard,

once, twice, to let her know
I understand, a Morse code,

telling her I understand, and she grips
my hand back, once, twice,

a message received and understood.
My heart wings in the rhythm

of a scared hen, thrashing against
the henhouse when a wolf circles it outside.

THE MORNING

The sun rises. We have been walking
        for many hours through the fields

on a dirt road. No one is saying
        a word as we walk

weighed down by worries,
        our backs bent lower

and lower with each step we take
        away from home. And the sun is like

an eye in the sky, watching us.
        We can't hide anywhere.

Back home, chickens must be
        waiting for us to feed them

and no one is left.
        No one is home.

PEELING LAYERS LIKE ONIONS

The backpack digs into my shoulders.
I am sweating in my coat,

and when I take it off,
about to throw it on the ground

like others have done, coats and jackets
and bags and food littered behind us,

leaving behind a trail for anyone to follow.
Auntie—her face flushed like a red onion—

tells me to carry it,
because we will need it.

She tells Asa never to let go of her coat,
never to let go of my hand. Ever.

Halting for a Rest

Principal Ohara raises his arm and we halt.
We stop. We sigh. We drop our bodies
wherever we are, with packs still

on our backs, and close our eyes.
My feet hurt. My legs feel heavy,
like I'm dragging the weight of two logs.

Asa presses next to me and I put my arm
around her body. Auntie sits next
to Asa and opens her backpack.

"Eat," she says, and holds out a rice ball.
I shake my head. I can't even tell
her I'm too tired to eat, but she says

that if I don't eat now, I won't be
able to walk, and she pinches off
a piece with her thick wrinkly fingers

and tells me to open my mouth.
I open my mouth slowly, and she feeds
me a piece, then another to Asa,

and another to herself.
And we chew slowly like cows,
rolling the pieces inside our mouths,

and I don't know
what I'm chewing so tired I am,
and I close my eyes.

THIS IS A DREAM

Asa snuggles next to me,
her body shaped around my own.

Next to me Tochan snores
like a bullfrog, lifting up the blanket

every time he exhales. I hear the hens
clucking in the yard and Horse hoofing

the barn ground, trying to wake
us up. And I smell Kachan,

her hand touching my arm,
Wake up, Natsu, my little summer.

Then I open my eyes,
and we are on the hard and dusty road,

surrounded by other people lying
this way on their sides or that way

on their backs, our bodies confused
arrows pointing true and false norths.

And I know:
this is not a dream.

A Dried Apple Candy

Asa trips over an invisible
rock and I stumble along,
my feet hurting from blisters.

My steps are heavier, slower.
People pass by us
as I struggle along,

my shoulders hurting from the straps.
Auntie tugs my hand,
"Don't get behind. Keep walking,

keep walking," she says,
and I want to tell her I'm doing
my best, I'm walking as fast

as I can, but with each step
it's harder and heavier.
Asa stops in mid-step,

"I can't walk no more. I'm tired."
And I tell her that we'll be *there*
soon, though I don't know where *there* is.

"When we get there," I say,
"Tochan'll be there
with candies, I promise.

Tochan said that he's going
to wait for us there."
And Asa peers up at me

like she always does when she knows
I'm lying, but this time I see
that she wants to believe me.

I look up. I see Auntie looking
at me like a cat measuring its prey,
not blinking, just staring,

then her face crinkles into laughs.
"Asa, I heard him say it, too.
He said that he'll meet us

with every kind of candy he can
find. We'll get there soon,"
and she pulls out a dried apple candy

from her bag. "See? Here's one. Take it."
And with that, Auntie closes
one eye, just like a cat,

a wink,
and a smile hovers on her lips,
as if to say, *Let's lie to her.*

As if to say, *That was easy.*

A BUCKET FULL OF WATER

The dark clouds roll
over the sky,
pushing the blue aside

and the heaven and earth collide.
The ink-dark sky breaks open
and rain pours down

as if someone turned
a bucket full of water
upside down.

No one stops.
No one looks up.
We keep walking

with our heads down,
one step, then another.
We take steps

as if we are underwater,
our legs heavy,
our feet caught in mud.

The rain falls on us
like stones, rain bruises
our already bruised hearts

and makes us bow
our heads as if we've already
lost something important,

like home, like war,
like a thing so important
that we have to apologize for it.

THE UNBLINKING SUN

The sun breaks into the rain
and the rain stops as if on command,
like Horse halting with the cluck of my tongue.

One minute we were freezing in rain.
Another, we are boiling, sweat pouring down
our faces and our backs

and even our arms and legs.
Flies suck on our salty backs.
Flies bite into us.

The sun is an eye in the sky, watching us.
Toshio's mother takes off her coat
and we trample on it.

Principal Ohara takes off his jacket
and we step on it.
One layer, another layer,

stripping like bamboo skins.
The sun beats on us.
Like the unforgiving eye,

like Auntie watching me.
The ground hardens
and turns into shards of glass

cutting through our shoes,
cutting our feet into ribbons.
There is pain from the inside.

From the outside, too.
The blisters pop.
Auntie slows down to pick up

the coat Asa threw down.
She looks at me,
asks me if I'm doing okay.

I nod. I lie and nod.
Lying is the only thing
that's become easy.

THE HUNGRY NIGHT

The night swallows us
into the dark,
into the southern

landscape
with the blanket
of stars above us.

Our breaths white
against the dark
like cotton candy.

The cold rises
from the earth,
hungry ghosts looking for us.

EACH STEP A WAY TOWARD SAFETY

The darkness is long, measured by halting steps.
My feet burn, each step more painful
than the step before, and I trip from pain,

from an invisible root. Auntie slows down.
Asa, half-asleep, stops. Auntie takes
a pink sash from her bag and ties one end

to her backpack, strings it through
Asa's buttonhole, and ties the end
to my backpack. "Don't slow down, ever.

We can never separate, not from each other,
not from the group," she says sternly,
and I hate her stinging words,

but I also know that she is telling the truth.
If we ever lose our way here, we will never
be able to find our way toward the garrison,

and this is also the truth: the three of us,
our lives are as one, and if we lose one another,
we each will be lost without the others.

HEART AS DARK AS THE NIGHT

Asa wilts in our chain of three.
"I'm tired," she whispers,
her words falling out

of her mouth so slowly
that she sounds
like she's half-asleep.

I'm tired, too, but
I don't say anything.
"I'm tired," Asa repeats,

louder this time,
and someone ahead
of us hisses in the darkness,

"Shut the brat up."
My mouth opens
to talk back, but I hear

Auntie click her tongue
and say quietly,
"Forget it, Natsu,

save your energy."
My arm feels so heavy
but I lift it and put my hand

on Asa's shoulder and squeeze
it once, twice. *It's going
to be okay, I'm here.*

I take one step, then another.
Asa starts to walk
again, slowly, her steps small.

In this darkness, the farther away
we are from home,
the more people become

meaner and meaner,
the light in their hearts
getting small and smaller

until they are extinguished,
their hearts as dark as the night,
as hard as this ground we walk on.

The Burning Hearts

Chickens and pigs run
around. Smoke comes
out of chimneys.

Dirty dishes in a pail.
But so quiet. No one is about
in this Manchu hamlet.

It's as if the world has stopped,
and the only people
who are alive are us.

Then suddenly,
doors burst open,
men, women, and children

with pitchforks,
brooms, big machetes,
their anger cracking

the air like oncoming
thunder, and we shrink
as one, huddling closer

to one another,
a ball of a dozen and a half
of us, shrinking.

"*Riben Guizi! Riben Guizi!*"
Japanese devils! Japanese devils!
they chant, and they begin

to tighten the circle,
and Principal Ohara says,
"Stay close to the group.

Don't say anything.
Don't move too quickly!"
as the chant gets closer

and they get closer
and he says something
quickly in Chinese,

rapidly, raising both his hands
in the air, moving forward.
He says something

again and again,
motioning us to keep
moving, to keep moving,

our arms raised as one,
in surrender, to show
that we mean them no harm.

My heart beats fast.
The principal keeps saying something
very fast, and we keep moving

through the small hamlet fast,
faster in one tight ball, until
we are out of the hamlet

and the villagers
stand by the edge
glaring at us.

They never put
down their weapons
and we keep our arms up

even when we can't see
them anymore
and they can't see us.

But I can still feel
their hatred and anger
burning red-hot,

and it's as mysterious
as how the heart keeps beating
even after fear is gone.

THE HEART KEEPS BEATING, OUR FEET KEEP MOVING

We keep moving.
We keep moving

in fear,
walking fast,

walking faster.
"Stop," the principal says.

"We can stop now."
But my legs want

to keep moving,
I am so scared.

I want to go away.
I can't stop moving.

My throat is parched.
No matter how much I lick

my lips, they dry up.
Then I stop.

Only my heart keeps
beating fast and faster

and it would have kept
going and going

if it weren't for my feet
that have stopped moving.

THE EMPEROR'S CHILDREN

"Listen carefully," the principal says.
"Listen, this is important," he says.

"We are in a hostile area and
we are extremely vulnerable

with no men and only women and children.
We must take precautions,

just like we talked about
during the drills."

All the women in the group nod.
All the older girls in the group nod.

I look around, I look to Auntie,
and without saying a word,

she nods and opens her bag.
All around me, women open

their bags to look for something.
Auntie pulls out a knife.

She looks at me.
"I'm so sorry," she says.

I remember all the stories of wives
of samurais who killed

themselves rather than surrender
to the enemy. Isn't this what Japanese

women are supposed to do?
Isn't this what we've been taught

to do for His Majesty the Emperor?
We will die for him,

and *we* Japanese are brave,
we are courageous. *We* do not fear death.

I am Japanese. I am courageous.
I do not fear death. I close my eyes.

Asa presses herself
against me.

"I don't want to die," she whispers.
I'm scared. I'm scared to die.

I'm scared but I have to be brave.
I nod. I'm ready.

I feel Auntie's hand on my neck.
I feel the cold blade

of the knife touching my nape.
I hang my neck.

"I'm so sorry," Auntie whispers,
and I close my eyes tighter.

Rhythm of the Harvest

My neck feels colder,
and something falls
onto the ground.

I slowly open my eyes.
There, by my knees,
the thick braid.

Then the hacking sound,
and another braid
falls to the ground.

She hacks strand after strand
of hair close to my skull.
I can feel the wind

passing over my head.
I can feel the wind
curving around my neck.

All around me, sounds similar
to the wheat being hacked off
during the harvest, one hack

calling to another,
a call-and-response.
All around me, black hair,

loose hair falls
onto the ground, then swirls up,
down, scattered by the wind.

WE SAT DOWN AS GIRLS, WE RISE AS MEN

We smear mud
on our faces.

We smear mud
on our hands and ankles.

Women bind their breasts
with sashes to flatten their chests.

Men do awful things to women,
Auntie whispers.

If we look like men, they'll hopefully
leave us alone.

Asa looks up, her head as bald
as a newborn chick's;

I take a handful
of mud and smear it on her cheek,

first, left, then right
She takes a fistful of mud

and smears it on my cheek,
then we can't stop.

We are back in the settlement
and smiling and almost laughing.

Auntie, her hair shorn like an old man's,
looks at me, then breaks into a grin.

I kneeled down as a girl.
I stand up and walk

as if I were a boy
fearing nothing.

PART THREE

END OF SUMMER

The Broken Bridge

The roaring. The grumbling earth.
I look up at the sky but it is empty.

I look around and I see it,
a river, pregnant with yesterday's rain,

brown and furious, and the bridge stretches
halfway into the river, then disappears.

A rope runs across the surface, with one end
tied to a tree on the other bank.

One by one, our neighbors open
their bags, pulling this or that to lighten the load

and once the bags are closed,
step into the river, one by one, holding on

to the rope, holding on to
their lives, one by one.

THE FIRST STEP

Auntie glares at the river
threateningly, as she has
glared at me

when I kicked her chickens
or stuck my tongue out at her.
She stands firm,

her legs apart,
her arms in the stance
of the gunfighter.

This is it. This is the river.
We need to cross.
"Are you ready?"

And I nod, and Asa nods.
I pull Asa to me
and hoist her up

so her arms are around
my neck and her legs
around my waist.

Auntie ties the sash
around Asa and me.
Then she pulls a new sash out

and ties it around her waist,
then ties the other end
around my waist.

"Don't let go of each other
no matter what.
If we go down,

we go together, you hear?"
She roars above the river,
and she holds the rope,

and I hold the rope,
and she looks back—
Are you ready?

I am ready. I nod.
I take a step,
this one different.

The Crossing

The current sweeps
under me,

and my left foot slips
on a rock,

and I hold on
with both my hands.

Asa's arms tighten
around me

and I hear Auntie say,
"Hold on. Hold on."

One step, finding
the solid footing

with my left foot
while I shift

my right foot forward.
The river gorges,

swallowing,
sucking my feet

into its vortex,
angry at us,

angry at the sky.
A big broken tree shoots

through the water
in front of me.

I take another step.
Then another.

Asa presses her face
against my shoulder

and the backpack is pulled
this way, that way

by the current.
Auntie moves waist-deep,

and the water comes to my chest,
ripping, gripping,

throwing me around.
I take another

step, my hands numb
from the cold,

my legs heavy
as if I am dragging stones

around my ankles,
but I take another step.

Toshio's mom screams
up ahead,

then is swept away,
her head appearing,

disappearing amid
the fast current.

I scream and water
enters my nose

and my mouth.
And Auntie screams,

and Toshio's mom's arm
bobs up

downstream,
then her face,

and "Help me, help me!"
and people on the other bank

try to reach out but can't.
"Help me, help me,"

I keep hearing,
or maybe I'm imagining it,

and Auntie roars,
"Almost there!"

And suddenly the river
sweeps my feet

from under me,
"Tochan, Tochan,"

I scream,
but water enters my nose,

and Asa screams,
"Natsu-chan, Natsu-chan."

The sash stops me and Asa,
Auntie holding on to the rope

with all her might.
"Hold on, hold on!"

Auntie's voice roars
above the river,

and I try to find
the sash underwater.

There, the sash.
Asa goes underwater

then up, my head goes
under, then up

and my throat burns.
"Almost. You have to pull

yourself, I can't let go
of the rope!" I think Auntie

yells, Auntie's lips blue
and I pull at the sash

one arm at a time,
one at a time,

until I can reach
the rope

and Auntie pulls me
to her with one arm

and I hear people yelling,
"Keep going, keep going,"

and I take a step,
then another,

Asa's arms around me,
never taking my eyes

off of Auntie's shaved head
until the river gets

shallower and shallower
and my feet stronger

and stronger
and the current weaker

and weaker
and we collapse

on the bank
in one big ball,

Auntie, Asa, and I, alive.
We are alive.

TO LIVE

I can't feel my hands.
I can't feel

my legs. My teeth chatter
and I can't do

anything to stop them.
Asa presses her face

close to me. Her lips are blue
like Kachan's were

when she died,
and Auntie, holding me,

is ice-cold. The cloth is heavy
and colder than any snow

I've ever known,
as if I am wearing

a coat made out of ice.
Late autumn in Manchuria

is hot during the day,
cold in the afternoon,

and can be like winter at night.
I can't stop shaking.

I can't stop trembling.
But I remember:

Tochan said that if I am ever
caught up in a thick blinding

blizzard outside the settlement
and I can't find my way home,

to never close my eyes.
Rub my hands. Rub my legs.

Stomp my feet, keep moving.
Keep my blood flowing.

Don't ever give up
but keep going.

Keep moving my body
even if it means I am

walking farther and farther
away from home.

To Keep Moving, to Keep Moving to Stay Alive

We need to keep walking
to stay warm,
to get to Harbin.

We need to keep walking
to stay alive,
to get to safety.

We need to keep walking
to get away from the Soviets,
to get away from the Chinese.

We need to keep walking.
We must keep walking
so we can stay

alive for a little longer.

NIGHTS ARE DAYS, DAYS ARE NIGHTS

Nights are days, days are nights,
and we keep walking one step at a time.

It feels like three days,
it feels like a lifetime,

my home feels like a dream.
I don't know how long we've been walking.

Asa lies heavy on my back,
trusting all her weight to me.

Auntie staggers ahead, her back bent
low as the wheat heads must be back home,

heavy for harvest, heavy for bounty.
Asa stirs, then wriggles.

"Shhh, go back to sleep," I tell her.
She slides down my back

like a cat sliding off a tree.
"Natsu-chan, I can walk.

I don't want you to get tired."
Instead, we hold hands,

her hand squeezing
mine, sending me

the Morse code, the only thing
that is real right now

because I don't know where
I am, I don't know anything anymore.

The Rest

We sit as one.
No one has anything
left to eat,

even our stomachs
have forgotten about us.
We've been carrying empty

canteens for so many days,
and we've been swallowing
spit in our mouths.

We don't know if we are
hungry or thirsty or tired.
We just lie there,

in damp clothes,
hoping that a train
will come this way,

an army truck, maybe,
to take us south.
Hoping that someone

—anyone—
will find us,
because we can't take

one more step.
We have no steps
left in us.

CRUMBS

"Eat," Auntie holds out
a dried apple candy

the size of a pinkie.
"This is the last one."

Asa takes it,
puts it in her mouth

greedily, then looks
at me, then Auntie.

She pulls it out.
"What about you?"

she asks. Auntie shakes
her head. I shake my head.

My stomach grumbles weakly
like a distant thunder.

Asa looks from Auntie
to me. Then she pinches

a sliver, then another,
and gives them to me and Auntie.

The apple, already soft, spreads
in my mouth, and melts,

reminding me of home
and Tochan and Horse.

The Starred Wings

A drone buzzes far away,
and I shake my head

to ward it off.
It continues.

A fly buzzes,
or is it something else?

Then there's a glint
in the sky

coming closer and closer,
a lone plane.

"A Japanese plane,"
someone cheers,

and we all look up.
A plane comes closer,

we wave our arms.
"We're safe! We're safe!"

Then other planes come
from the northern sky

in formation like a flock
of silver geese.

The first plane zooms
past us bearing a red star

under its wing.
"Run for cover. Run for cover,"

Principal yells.
A red star, not a red sun.

"The Soviets, run for cover!"
and before I can think,

I throw myself
onto the ground

like a ball,
and all around me,

the road explodes,
pop, pop, pop,

to the left of me,
to the right of me.

Left, the earth is exploding,
and bullets riddle the ground.

Bags and people flying up, up,
then down, spinning

and whirling.
And Mr. Mishima

from two houses down,
dances like a puppet,

jerking his arm up,
his legs kick up,

dancing out of rhythm,
and I scream

—or maybe I don't—
and as if someone had cut the strings,

Mr. Mishima collapses
right in front of me.

And I scream
—or maybe I don't—

and after forever,
after forever and ever,

the drones are gone
and silence turns

into screams.
Mama! Yoko!

Masa! Aiko!
And Mr. Mishima lies there,

in front of me,
staring at me

though he no longer
sees me.

My voice is gone
but my mouth keeps moving

Asa! Auntie! Tochan!
Kachan! I don't want to die!

And my voice is gone
and I am gone.

UNSEEING EYES

And I hear. And I hear
someone calling out,

"Natsu! Natsu!"
I slowly raise my head

and there, two pairs of legs,
one with leather

shoes, and another barefoot.
I look up, following the legs,

and there Asa stands
huddled, holding on to

Auntie's waist,
and Auntie pulls me up gently.

"Are you hurt? Are you all right?"
When I nod,

her face relaxes, then
a smile of relief reaches her eyes.

"Help me find my sandals."
I want to nod.

I want to say yes,
but nothing comes out

of my mouth
and my body starts

to shake uncontrollably,
though I am not cold.

My hands are twitching
and jerking like Mr. Mishima,

and he still lies there,
near us, with his eyes still wide

open and his mouth opened
wider as if he is about to scream.

I close my eyes
though I keep seeing

Mr. Mishima's eyes
staring into mine without seeing.

Asa sneaks into my arms,
her heart beating fast

and my heart joins hers, beating
in the same erratic beats.

DON'T LOOK

"Don't look," Auntie barks.
"Just go into the field

and look for my shoes,"
she growls as she gathers

spilled contents from my bag:
the tablet, papers, pouches,

and as if I have come
out from underwater,

voices, voices everywhere.
I hurt, I hurt. Mama, mama!

Masako, don't die!
The chorus of voices

all cacophony of voices,
sadness, pain,

so thick I taste it in my mouth,
the metallic taste of blood.

And Auntie pulls me
to her big chest,

covering my eyes,
"Don't look, Natsu!"

I pull Asa
into my chest,

"Don't look, Asa,
don't you dare look."

THE TURTLE ELDER MAN

Auntie and I carry
Principal Ohara's wife,
bleeding from her thigh

and arm, leaving a trail
of blood behind her,
and Asa carries a baby

on her back,
the baby without her mother.
We walk and walk,

led by the principal,
our march of the dead,
until we make it

finally to a Manchu hamlet.
We see smoke coming out of a chimney.
Chickens running around

the compound. My heart starts beating
fast: this is not the village we passed
by. But I remember the anger.

Huts huddling together
as if they are scared.
My heart flutters like a caged hen.

An old man comes out
of a dirty hut, walking
slowly like a turtle

from its shell and looks at us
as if he is scared.
I can feel eyes,

but I can't see
anyone. Two dozen
or so of us,

without bags, hungry,
covered in blood
not our own, or our own.

The principal slowly puts
down his sable,
then raises his arms,

almost in the gesture of surrender,
and he says slowly in Chinese,
"Some of us are hurt,

can you help us?"
The Turtle Elder Man blinks
slowly, and the eyes watch

us, and we hold our breath
as they must be holding
their breath, and slowly

the Turtle Elder Man says,
"Yes, yes," slowly as if chewing
his words like food.

"Yes, bring your wounded here
and we will take care of them,
and you can rest for a while."

He says slowly,
"There have been many Japanese passing
here in groups lately.

It seems that things
are not safe anymore."
The principal bows deeply.

We all bow, as low as we can,
as if to say, *We won't hurt you,*
please, please don't hurt us.

My heart stops its fluttering
and the hen settles down
to preen itself in my chest.

ALMOST A HOME

We divide up, the dead
left on the ground,
the wounded taken

to the Turtle Elder Man's hut,
and the rest to different houses.
Auntie, Asa, and I are led

to a house near the edge
of the hamlet, a cold
and dark hut that smells of oil

and earth and sleep
and exhaustion
where a father, a mother,

a grandmother, and five children
live with pigs and chickens.
It is crowded, it is dark,

but they give us warm water
that tastes like tea from yesterday,
and hot bowls of sorghum gruel.

We drink them down
like it is a feast
fit for the Imperial family, and it is.

The grandmother brings
over heated water and torn
cloth and beckons us

to wash ourselves
by moving her hands
in front of her face.

Soon enough,
we feel warm from our stomachs
for the first time in a while,

and soon enough,
we feel less sweaty,
and soon enough,

Asa and the kids are laughing
and chattering like hens in spring
and I feel safe for the first time in days.

When the Words Aren't Enough

The sky bursts into explosions of red
turning everything bloody,
and as soon as the sky darkens,

the call to gather and leave comes
all too soon. Auntie sighs, gets up,
puts on her coat, and opens

her backpack. She rummages
around and pulls out a wooden statue
of Kannon and hands it to the father.

"Thank you, thank you,"
she says in Chinese and Japanese,
bowing deeply, and Asa and I repeat

after her, but the father pushes
the statue back at Auntie.
She tries to give him the statue again,

and the father pushes it back again,
and he says, "It was the least
we can do for people who needed help."

We all bow deeply. "Thank you. Thank you,"
because that's the only thing we can say,
because we mean it more than we can say.

THE TRACK AT THE END OF THE WORLD

The railroad track that would take us south
to Harbin lies lonely amid the golden plain,

and we sigh in relief. All is quiet as if it doesn't care
about us, those of us who have just walked

those miles and miles from the other side
of the horizon to get here.

UNDER THE BROKEN SKY

The sun slowly dries my wet clothes,
as I lie on my back. The sky is so high
that even when I reach up, I can't touch

it; I can't feel it. The blue is so deep
indigo with not a cloud in the sky, but it is
broken, just like us. It is indifferent.

It doesn't care whether we move
or we die on the ground so far down
from where it is. The sky is empty.

No clouds. No birds.
Just a blue sheet of sky that doesn't care
what happens on the ground.

I want to take a sword, or a spear,
or the gun in my pack and shatter its
indifference into smithereens.

THE RUMBLING SKY

The ground rumbles.
The ground moans.
I jerk up

from the sleep
I didn't know I had fallen
into. I sit up,

and all around,
I see heads popping
up like rabbits'.

Auntie's head,
Asa's, the principal's,
our neighbors'.

The earth rumbles.
The sky seems to tremble.
I look around,

and there, a locomotive
chugging slowly
toward us.

We all jump up.
We all get on the track,
waving our arms

to flag it down.
The engine car passes
us, one cattle car

after another,
until the train comes
to a halt,

and we all limp
toward the door.
The door slides open,

and inside, it's filled with
Japanese settlers—
women and children—

just like us,
huddling so tightly
there is no space

for us to join them.
Someone from the car yells,
"Jump in. We can't stop here too long.

Jump in quickly,"
and the principal pushes
people in, one by one,

as someone pulls people
in, one by one.
Asa gets pushed up

and she disappears
into the dark car.
A hand pulls me up

and I stumble next
to Asa, and after me
comes Auntie.

Then someone slams
the door shut.
The horn hoots once,

then again,
and the car trembles,
and the train chugs

forward and I collapse
against the wall.
We are safe.

THE END OF THE WORLD

I don't know who said it first.
        I don't know who started it first.

But someone in the car said
        that Japan has surrendered.

That Japan has lost the war.

That the Emperor himself
        made the announcement
                three days ago or sometime ago, they don't know.

That Manchuria is overrun
        with the Soviets or the Nationalists
                or the Communists; they aren't sure.

That the tracks all over Manchuria
        have been bombed and destroyed,
                and this is the only line
                        that hasn't been blown up,
                                or so they think.

That the Americans dropped this new
        bomb and completely destroyed
                the motherland, and the only person still
                        alive is the Emperor.

That Japan has surrendered.

That nothing is left of Japan.

That the Japanese Army by the border
made their last charge and all died honorably.

It's a lie, I know.

Japan would never surrender.
The Emperor would never surrender.
Japan has never lost a war,
never in its 2,605-year history.

It's a lie, I know.

No one can kill Tochan, not him, never.
The Wind of Gods will blow,
bringing victory to us as it has done
so many times in the past.

People lie.

They are lying. These are all lies.

Japan didn't lose.

These people are lying.

The Emperor would never surrender.

These people are lying.

The Wind of Gods would
        have come to bring victory
                like it has so many times before.

                These people are lying.

                        It must be a lie.
        It must be a lie.

I keep telling myself,
        but somehow, somewhere I know
                it must be true.
                        We are here, aren't we?
        Away from home.
Running away from home.

The Empty Heart

I sit against
the slotted wall,
holding my knees
close to me.

Auntie is asleep
and so is Asa,
sleeping with her
mouth open.

The car is filled
with women and children
like Auntie and Asa.
Dirty, tired, and no one

says a word
as the car rumbles
in the rhythm
of the train chug.

Someone says that
this is the last train
going south,
that this is the evacuation

train driven by men
who went against
the Japanese Army
to rescue stranded *civilians*.

That this is one
of the very few rail lines
not destroyed by
the army on their retreat.

The landscape passes
by slowly with the speed
of the crawling train,
a never-ending

field of gold,
empty as the sky,
and emptier
than my heart.

HOME IS NO LONGER HERE

I watch the golden prairie
glide past the slow-moving train.

I look over, and Auntie is looking
at me like a cat staring at a mouse.

"So Japan lost the war," she says
under her breath. My eyes sting,

and I look away. "Well, we won't be going
home anytime soon," she says.

My mind becomes fuller with questions
than anger. "What do you mean,

we can't go home?" I ask.
"Exactly that. We can't go back

to the settlement, not ever,
now that Manchuria's gone."

Isn't this Manchuria?
Or did it disappear when the war ended?

ANGRY HEART

The Chinese villagers
who chased after us
with pitchforks,
their anger so loud

you could hear it cracking.
The Chinese watermelon
thief who said that
Japan was going to lose

the war. Every morning
we bowed to the east,
where His Majesty the Emperor
lives. Every morning, we recited

our allegiance to the Emperor.
The special forces pilots
who dived into the enemy
ships, sacrificing their lives

to save us. All the soldiers
who made their last charges,
in Saipan, in Iwo Jima,
in the Aleutian Islands.

All the letters I had written to
soldiers telling them to die
honorably. And we worked
all day on the farm,

being told that it was
for Japan, and we worked
so hard. And most of all,
Tochan, taking his old rifle

and riding Horse.
And all these men
we sent off that day
with us waving Japanese flags

made by Toshio's mom
like it was a festival day.
What was all of this for?
Why did it all happen?

RABBITS ON THE PLAIN

The train slows down then stops.
The door slides open

letting the blinding light
in, blinding me, and after a pause,

shadows get up
here and there,

and people jump out of the train
to go into the field

to relieve themselves.
Before anyone is back,

the engineer pulls
the horn, and the train begins

to move, and people come
popping up from the field like rabbits

and run toward the moving
train, some with their pants

around their legs,
and the train moves faster and faster

and they reach out their hands
but no one can grab

their hands and we leave
them behind as the train keeps

moving
south toward Harbin.

HARBIN

The landscape changes from empty plain
to a house, then a cluster of houses,

as the roads become paved and trees thin.
The houses flash by. Houses made out

of red bricks, getting taller and taller
until we slide into a platform

covered with people and the train comes
to a halt. The door slides open,

and the voices sing out, *Harbin.*
Harbin. Harbin. Someone will

tell me that Japan has won the war.
Someone will tell me that we can go home.

And Tochan will be there.
When we get home.

The End of the Forever Reign

We walk like obedient sheep, dragging
our feet without saying a word.

The Chinese walk the streets with tattered
flags of Manchuria, tearing down

Japanese signs and coming out
of stores with arms full of goods.

They jeer at us. They spit as we walk
by, and Principal Ohara tells us, "Run, run."

Auntie grabs my hand and I grab
Asa's hand and we run, run, like scared sheep,

following the group. We run, run
through the streets and across the streets

to a former Japanese girls' school
where the hallways are packed

with scared people like us, dirty
and tired-looking like us, until we go into a room

already filled with people from a different settlement.
They look up in fear when we enter,

and relax as soon as they see we are Japanese,
tired and scared like them.

We drop our bags
and collapse onto the coldest

hardest floor and fall asleep like eternal rocks.
The ten-thousand-year reign

of the Emperor ended some days ago,
and we didn't even know it.

We are no longer the Emperor's children.
We are orphaned.

PART FOUR

BEGINNING OF AUTUMN

THIS IS NOT A DREAM

I stand outside our house and it is still
the same wall made out of mud and straw,

the roof is thatched. There are the chickens,
white, black, and white-pebbled, pecking on seeds.

I hear Goat in the barn jumping her joyful
jumps, and Horse eating hay. Then the door opens

and Tochan walks out with a handgun.
I ask him why he's holding the gun. Is there trouble?

But it comes out in Chinese, and he looks at me
like he's never seen me, and raises the gun

and tells me to stop where I am.
And I tell him, "It's me. It's Natsu. I'm your daughter,"

but it comes out in Chinese and he looks scared
and tells someone inside to stay there.

I see myself peeking out from behind him,
and I tell him, "I'm Natsu. That's not me. Who is that?"

and he raises the gun and I shield my face, and the gun goes off
and I feel hot pain in my shoulder. I wake up screaming.

I am in a dark room. Auntie lies snoring, holding on
to her backpack, and Asa asleep between us,

curled up, her thumb in her mouth, and I still have
my arms around the tired backpack.

AUGUST 1945

"When can we go home?" I ask Auntie.
The sorghum gruel feels like barbed wire
going down my throat.
Auntie shakes her head.

She swallows the gruel from the bowl,
and crinkles her face.
"Natsu, we can't," she says between each chew,
as if she's choosing her words

carefully. "If the war is over,
then we can go home, Tochan
and Taro are probably already home," I say.
Auntie puts down the metal bowl

on the uneven wooden floor.
My stomach growls like a frog in summer.
Asa looks at her own half-eaten bowl.
"Natsu-chan, you can have my gruel.

I'm full," and when I reach out,
Auntie slaps my hand, "Asa, eat your food.
Natsu, don't be greedy." Then she says
slowly, her mouth moving to one side,

"I don't think our homes are waiting for us
anymore from all that I've heard,"
as she licks the last of the gruel
still in the bowl. "We might be

here for a long time, until we can get
home to Japan." But what about our home
up north? Our wheat, chickens, and all
that Tochan *worked toward* for so many years?

What about your plum trees
and your home, Auntie?
But I keep my mouth shut.
My stomach growls in protest.

SHADOWS IN THE ROOM

The Emperor did not stop
Tochan from being drafted
to leave us and go fight up north.

No one came to save us
while we were running
away from home.

No one reached out
to help Toshio's mom
from being swallowed by the river.

The divine wind did not blow
to push away the enemy airplane
when it started gunning us down.

No one sees us sitting here in the dark
classroom where the cold air enters
through the slots of the hard floor

and we sleep chilled to the bone,
where babies cry at all hours,
and adults sit in shadows hiding.

No one is going to rescue us.
No one is going to help us.
I now know. No one is going to help.

We are alone.

THE ARRIVAL OF RUSSIANS

The ground shakes and trembles.
Window frames rattle.
Russian soldiers in their tanks,

their jeeps and trucks,
their black boots shiny
like their machine guns

and medals and red emblems
of gold hammer and sickle,
they are here,

bringing with them
a hint of winter.
They enter, one regiment

at a time, proud,
thousands and millions of boot
heels slamming down

on the pavement as one.
The Chinese wave the red flags
with the hammer and sickle,

tearing down the Rising Sun flags
from the poles and trampling on them,
happy that the city is no longer

under Japanese rule,
while we watch
from the schoolroom,

holding our breath.
My arm around Asa tightens,
and her arm around me

becomes tighter and tighter,
"Is it going to be okay?" Asa whispers.
What is going to happen to us?

STORIES PEOPLE CARRY

More and more people arrive carrying tales of what happened
during their escape: a settlement west of us took

their own lives like we were supposed to,
Never surrender to the enemy. Die honorably.

A girl survived, and she still wraps a thick bandage
around her neck because her mother loved her too much

and didn't stab her deeply enough, and another settler group
found her amid dead bodies, still alive, but barely.

Another settlement made it as far as the river where we crossed,
but they had to leave the sick and the old and the young behind

so they could pass the river without hindrance. They say
that it was the Japanese Imperial Army that blew up the bridge

so that the Soviets couldn't follow south. Settlers like us
were caught between the river and the Soviets, and we were told

we were lucky because the river wasn't as flooded as it had been
    the days before.
Another settlement was run over by Soviet tanks.

And one person saw the families of officers and the
    Manchurian Railway
leaving on planes with their furniture and bags three weeks

before the Surrender. They must have known that this was
    a lost war,
laughing and waving their hands as we settlers had to crawl
    through mud

and fear, hiding during the day and walking in the darkness just to get help from the army that had already left.

We are so many here, with tales, with stories, and mine isn't the worst.

UNINVITED GUESTS

The Soviets come inside
without knocking,
breaking down the barriers
and locked doors.

We turned in our guns
and swords, our scissors
and razors.
Tochan's gun

went with them.
Then they returned
demanding watches
and rings and if anyone

refused, the soldiers struck
them with the butts of
their rifles. Then they told
all the men to raise their arms

and get into the truck.
Principal Ohara was one of them.
He told us not to worry.
He told us he'd be back soon.

He walked out of the sixth-grade room,
as if he were still a principal
leading students out to the yard,
his hands in the air, and he got

on the back of the truck with the other men,
and we watched him from
the window until the truck
went through the school gate,

until it turned and disappeared
into the city. We waited for them
for hours to come back, but they never did.
And in the early morning, we heard gunshots.

I whisper to trembling
Asa, "Shhhh, it's okay, it's like
firecrackers." We hear the noises
of trucks and jeeps and gunshots

and gunshots and gunshots.
"Shhh, it's okay, it's only firecrackers,"
I tell Asa trembling in my arms,
and my heart keeps pounding,

it's going to explode soon.

Empty Promise

There is no Emperor
who can save us.

There is no Japanese
Imperial Army

who can protect us.
There is no one

who can reach over
and pull us out

of this room.
It is up to me

to protect
Auntie and Asa.

It is up to me
to take Asa back

to Japan
because there is no home

anymore for us here.
Because I promised Tochan.

And Tochan promised
that he will come find us

no matter where we are,
he will find us.

But until then—until then
I have to be strong.

INSIDE OUT

The schoolhouse stands
like a skeleton without glass
in the window frames.

They have all been shattered
or taken away by the Chinese
or whomever had looted

the place by the time we arrived.
We try to cover the openings
with discarded newspapers

but the morning steals
into the room, newspapers become sodden
and fall from the windowpanes,

and the schoolhouse trembles
in the cold. Asa stands
in her summer shirt trembling

like a shorn sheep
and I put my arms around her,
wishing I were a blanket

or as big as Tochan.
We shiver together inside.
Inside and out.

MEAN HEARTS

It's as if everyone's heart has frozen with the cold air.
We fight over who cut through the meal line.
Someone yells about someone else's bigger
portion and a fight breaks out.

(I just want to put my hands against my ears.)

Auntie finds a bundle of papers and tells Asa
and me to wrap them around our feet,
wrap them around our legs, our bellies
to keep them warm, says this is what she did
growing up poor back in Japan. I pull off
Asa's shoes and the leather
crumbles apart like mud, her feet blistered
and toenails crusted with dried blood.
She whimpers. I tell her she was brave
for not crying, but she is crying now.
Someone tells her to shut up.
I tell *them* to shut up, and they tell *me*
to shut up, and I tell *them* to shut up.

(I just want to put my hands against my ears.)

A sick old lady in the corner of the room coughs
all night, and people yell at her that they need to sleep.
She tries to stop by burying her face into her thin shirt,
trying to mute her coughs as much as she can.
I want her to shut up, too. I am getting meaner
and colder as if the autumn air brought meanness
with it and I don't like it. I don't like myself.
The room could break into pieces it's so cold.

(I just want to put my hands against my ears.)

OUR NEW HOME

"Don't trust anyone here,"
Auntie says, taking our backpacks
every time we go use the bathroom outside.

On the first day, someone stole my coat.
Then a couple of days ago, they stole
Asa's broken shoes.

Yesterday, someone stole our space
and when Auntie told the new family
to move, they said no, no matter how much

Auntie and I yelled at them,
until finally Asa said, "Let them stay, please don't fight."
We moved into the janitor's closet.

It is like a henhouse, small and smelly
and dark, but I feel safe. Auntie says that here,
we'll be safe, and we'll be a lot warmer

than in the classroom. With the door closed
we live in darkness but this darkness is warmer
than the cold and other people, colder still.

ONLY A MONTH AGO

We could go to
the well pump
and get the clearest

coldest water
anytime we wanted.
Only a month ago,

we could eat fresh
vegetables. We could eat
bowl after bowl of rice

and the juiciest watermelon
just harvested
from our farm.

Now, a month later,
we are only allowed
two small cups of cold gruel

so raw it hurts to swallow.
It tastes so bad
my tongue curls.

HOPE

People say that the men who were drafted
were run down and completely destroyed
by the Soviets. People say that the men

who were drafted all surrendered
to the Soviets when they came,
but they were released immediately,

and are coming down south as we speak.
People say that the men who were drafted
didn't fight the Soviets, and are marching

south to fight the Soviets and release us.
People say that Japan didn't surrender,
that the Americans lost the war and we can

go home any day, any day now.
I know Tochan will come find us. I know.
I know he is coming to get us.

Who I Am

My name is Natsu Kimura.
My sister is Asa Kimura.
My birthday is July 27.

We are from the X settlement.
My father's name is Takashi Kimura.
I don't know where my father is,

he is serving in the Imperial Army.
Here is my family registry.
This is my aunt.

No, she is not my real aunt,
she is a neighborhood woman.
No, please don't separate us,

she's family, yes, she's family,
no, please, please, I was lying,
she is my aunt, my father's aunt.

Please, don't separate us,
she's tired from the long trek here,
that's why she's coughing.

Her name is Ume Mitsui . . .
She's the only family we have.
She really is my aunt.

WARNINGS

We are told:
Keep your hair short
and dress like a man.

We are told:
No woman should walk
by herself in the city.

We are told:
If the Soviets attack
you don't resist. Let them.

We are told:
There will be only two cups of gruel per day.
If you want more, you are on your own.

We are told:
Don't agitate the Chinese,
don't make them angry.

We are told:
You need to go find jobs
if you want to survive, you are on your own.

We are told:
Japan has lost the war.
There is no more Japan.

Hot Sweet-Bean Buns

The cold bites into my skin.
I have been walking around
asking for a job, any job.

I tell them that I am healthy
and that I'll do anything,
but they all shoo me away

like I am a stray dog.
I can't walk anymore. I am so tired.
I know how to ride Horse.

I know when the seasons change
by the smell in the air.
I know which watermelon

is ripe and what good soil is.
I know how to milk goats
without getting kicked.

I don't know how to make money in a city.
My stomach grumbles.
I sit on the freezing street

where the Soviet soldiers
walk around with three,
four watches each on their arms,

their faces already red
from drinking too much.
A mother wearing a fur coat

holds her daughter's hand,
the girl's velvet coat as shiny
as Horse's back.

The girl looks at me. Our eyes meet.
Then she looks away. I sit still
and look at the pavement.

"Little girl, go home," someone whispers,
and throws a penny in front of me.
I look up, the mother with the girl

stands in front of me,
"Are you Japanese?" she asks.
I nod, painfully, my face burning

in shame. *What would Tochan say*
if he could see me now?
Tochan always said

that I can't rely on others.
Someone else throws a coin,
then another, and in half an hour,

I have seven coins,
enough to buy some hot buns.
My face feels hot like that time I had

pneumonia and I dreamed
of flying over a desert. I push
that thought aside. I am the only one

who can come out and earn money.
This is a job, I tell myself. *This is a job*
like working in a field.

Like feeding the hens.
Like plowing the earth.
I am doing this for Asa and Auntie.

Just as Tochan came home
carrying a rifle and holding
dead rabbits by their ears,

I can go home now
with a bag of hot sweet-bean buns
that will burn the tops of our mouths.

HUNGER

All I can think about is food
as I sit on the street.

Piping hot gruel made out
of real white rice.

Pickled plums Auntie used
to bring over every autumn

after they'd been sitting
in the dark jar underground

for one year.
A fried rice ball

covered in soybean flour
with red sauce and sesame seeds.

Steamed minced pork bun
so hot to touch, too hot to bite into,

but worth feeling burned
anyway. Onion pancakes

stacked up on a tray.
The delicious smell feeds

my imagination, but my stomach
is not fooled by imagined bites.

ANOTHER SUCCESS

I go home with a swagger
like I used to,
when I went home

after winning the first prize
ribbons in a run meet.
I go home with a swagger,

and I enter the hallway
where Auntie and Asa are
mending our clothes by our door.

I pull out the bag of hot buns,
a week running now.
Asa claps her hands.

Auntie looks pleased
as she massages her swollen legs
that pain her every step she takes

even after weeks of resting.
I am proud. I can do this.
I know I can.

BEAUTIFUL ASA

People come and go
from the school,

like the birds making
their way north in spring

and their way south in autumn.
Asa comes back to our closet

with a thumb in her mouth,
"Mai-chan is gone."

"Mai-chan?" I ask,
and Auntie says

that she was Asa's friend
who lived in the Third Year's Room.

People come and go,
and Asa keeps making friends:

Mai-chan one week, Satoko-chan
two weeks ago, Tomo-kun yesterday,

and they keep disappearing
as if they are birds who are

on their way somewhere else
but not here to stay.

How Easy It Is to Beg

The best place to beg
is in front of the Soviet Army
barrack where they may

not like the Japanese,
but they feel sorry
for a kid like me.

I call out, "*Dawai, dawai,*"
and soldiers, tall with the eyes
of ice and big red noses,

look sadly at me
and give me what they can.
Sometimes Asa comes and

she begs with me,
sometimes I go alone
and I bring back coins.

Auntie stays in the closet
like a mole, or hibernating rabbit,
her legs still hurting.

I bring back half a loaf
of black bread
that one soldier gave me,

and I split it three ways:
Auntie, Asa, and me.
The black bread, sour and hard,

softens in my mouth,
and goes down in small bites,
filling me up slowly.

WINTER IS HERE

Snowflakes twirl
into the hallway,

into our closet room
through the opening

of the door, swirling
around the portrait

of the Emperor who used
to sit in the locked altar room

of my school back home,
his round glasses perched

uncomfortably on his nose.
He sits next to us,

facedown as we sit
in our little closet home,

but even now, nothing touches
him, not even the bone-breaking cold.

FORGETTING

More and more, I can't remember
my house by the northern border of the prairie.
I see the chickens. I see the well. I see
the bathtub. I see Horse standing by the stall

waiting for me to feed her in the morning.
I see our door and our windows.
I see the wooden table Tochan had made
when he and Kachan first moved to Manchuria.

I see the altar. But I can't remember the smell.
I can't remember Asa as she was back in August,
before all this; all I see is her sunken cheeks,
her bony legs like a newborn calf's, wobbly and thin.

I can't remember Auntie scolding me
because nowadays, she sits in the closet,
she can't walk too fast or too long
before her legs start hurting.

I can't remember what it feels like to be warm
on the floor where we three slept in the shape of the river.
As I sleep on the cold floor with Auntie and Asa,
our bodies are piled up like a ball of kittens.

FROZEN WATER

Water is as precious
as food here. The well
is iced over this morning.

We throw the portrait
of the Emperor into the fire
to melt the ice so we can drink

the water, so we can warm
ourselves. At least he's good
for something, finally.

THE SCHOOL

Each classroom is filled
to the brim with people like peaches

we'd eat from the can Tochan always ordered
for Asa on special days.

I walk down the hallway,
glass out of the panes,

and clothing dangles from the doorways,
from window frames and pegs

that students used to hang their coats.
The entire school smells

of latrines and Horse's dirty stall
and unwashed bodies

and bad breaths and stale-smelling hair.
People spill out from the doorways

to the hallway, people sleeping,
people eating and doing their stuff,

just like they would at home,
though we are so far away from home.

THE WAR ALREADY FORGOTTEN

The Chinese section of the city
does not remember there was war not
too long ago. Signs from restaurants hang

in many different colors and shapes:
blue for Muslims where they don't serve pork;
a gourd shape for where they sell

alcohol and men come out with red faces;
and a white udder shape for milk shops.
Sometimes, someone stops and whispers,

"Do you want to be my daughter?"
but I pretend I don't hear and run away.
And sometimes, if I stay long enough,

if I look sad enough, someone comes out
and gives me leftovers that I take
home. Asa's face lights up

like it used to back before all this,
Auntie looking at me like I did good.
We dive in like chickens during

feeding time, our thoughts only on food,
pecking and pecking
at the last little crumbs on the floor.

PART FIVE

LATE AUTUMN

A Ghost in the City

"Chi fan le ma? (Have you eaten well?)" a Chinese voice rings out.
"Yes, have you?" a voice calls back.
"Cigarettes! Cigarettes, anyone?" a Japanese voice yells.

"Here, boy, keep the change," a Russian voice replies.
"Japanese? Japanese? Japanese smart, very clean.
How much? How much?" I turn left at the marketplace

toward my favorite part of the city: the side streets,
where the city suddenly becomes narrow, cluttered, and dirty
full of smells and voices. Men sit on unevenly paved streets,

sucking on long-stemmed pipes. Chickens run around in flocks
while children run around with toys. Dogs lounge lazily on stone
steps and under tiled roofs. Voices call out to one another

from houses on both sides of the street, their faces invisible.
The smells of twisted ginger and bearded ginseng fills the streets,
and I feel alive like the dancing red Chinese characters waving

from signs above me. Here, an old man sells tea and spices,
his thin beard grown down to his chest.
All over the city, posters cover poles, on walls,

and on sides of buildings, posters with pictures
and a few words written in Russian, pictures of men
doing something, arrows pointing the way.

There, a storefront shop with baskets and baskets piled
on top of one another threatening to fall at any minute.
A woman selling Chinese pancakes slaps pieces

of dough against the hot stove, and when they fall on the ground,
the surface brown and cooked just right,
she slaps the other side until it, too, falls on the ground.

It's as if the war never touched these people,
not like it touched me. And I feel so alone,
as if I am a ghost who can't share my story with others.

BACK TO NORMAL

Auntie takes a basket
of clothing out of our closet
and sits in front of the door

with her bad legs thrown
in front of her.
"Never leave home without a sewing kit,"

she had said once, a long
time ago, "when I was a little girl,
clothing was more precious than food."

She takes a needle
and a thread, and mends a shirt
that has been mended too many times before.

Asa takes a newspaper
I had given to her, the one I found
on the street, and she starts

to draw a picture of a house.
I take out a book I found
in what used to be a school library

and open it; it's a book
about astronomy. Some words are
hard to read. But I read out loud

a page, then another, and another,
and Auntie mends and Asa keeps
drawing houses after another and another.

The air is cold. Our breath comes
out in white plumes. But the story of sun
keeps us warm, away from here.

I Look and I Don't Care

Men from the Japanese Community grab
the body by the ankles
and wrists carelessly, and carry it
down the hall and down the steps
toward the open pit. One, two, three,
they throw in the body.

(I look, and I don't care.)

The yard is covered with holes,
filled with frozen naked bodies.
A stiff pair of arms pokes
out of one of them
like two sunflower plants.

(I look, and I don't care.)

"Why aren't they buried?"
Asa asks, and turns away.
I tell her it's almost like
when Kachan died
and Tochan had to thaw the ground
with hot water because the earth
was frozen over with winter snow.

(I look, and I don't want to care.)

Hundreds and hundreds of bodies
—they looked more like lumber,
or plants, their bodies stiff
and pale and not at all like people.
Asa reaches over and slips her cold
hand into mine. "Promise me
you wouldn't just leave me
in a hole like that."

(I look, and I care.)

THIS IS HOW PEOPLE DIE

Quietly. In the night.
When no one is awake.
The dying close their eyes.
And in the morning,
they are dead.

The Deep of Winter

My nose runs and freezes
right as it comes out.
I have icicles for eyelashes,

and no matter how many times
I blink, my eyes water and freeze.
I stamp my feet but no one pays attention.

They bury their noses in fur
coats and walk hurriedly past me
and I have to move in order

to stay warm. I sure don't want
two bowls of that awful
sorghum gruel but winter has

frozen the hearts of people.
By the gate of the school,
a woman grabs my hand,

"Are you a Japanese boy?
Come home with me, I'll feed
you well, I'll treat you as my real son,"

she says in Chinese.
I push her hand away. So many
people like her outside the gate.

Why can't people just leave me alone?

SOMETIMES, WHEN I THINK OF HOME

I can't help it. It's always when
I am with Auntie and Asa.
It's always when we are sitting

together, telling one another
what has happened during our day.
Maybe Auntie says something

about someone from the settlement,
maybe it's Asa saying something
about a friend's parent who died,

my heart pangs, and I think of home.
Before I can stop myself,
my mouth starts to move,

and I start talking about Horse
and Tochan and hens and Goat
and Auntie's plum tree and the settlement

and the Wall. Auntie doesn't stop me
but lets me talk. Asa stops me
and tells me I'm remembering wrong.

I can't stop my mouth once I start.
I can't stop myself. I'm scared that if I
don't say these things, I'll start forgetting.

The Drunk Russian and His Wallet

I walk behind a Russian soldier.
His gait wavers, and he loses his footing

on the patch of ice, then rights himself.
Then I see it: his wallet is about to fall out

of his coat pocket. My heart pounds.
All I have to do is to reach over

and snatch the edge of his wallet and run.
That's all I have to do. I swallow, hard.

Then I dash, snatch his wallet,
and push him hard onto the sidewalk.

I run as fast as I can, through the streets,
running this way left, that way right.

I push people out of the way,
holding the wallet to my chest.

I run and run through the maze of shops.
And when I stop in a small alley,

my heart pounds. It's going to pop
out of my mouth. I open the wallet

to find many bills. I have stolen,
and it is so easy. When I show Auntie

the money, she looks at me hard,
without saying a word,

like she's trying to make me talk,
and I look away, as would a guilty dog,

"What would your *Tochan* say?"
she says quietly, and pulls me to her chest.

I know I will never steal again.
I don't want Auntie to be disappointed in me.

DISAPPEARING CHILDREN

As the icicles get thicker and bigger,
the voices outside of the gate
get louder and louder.

"Sell us your Japanese children!
Sell us your Japanese wives!
Japanese are strong and smart

and they are hard workers."
Russians look the other way.
They are soldiers. They don't need

wives or children.
And every day,
I see children disappear

in exactly that way:
mothers send their children
to Chinese men and women

who have no children
of their own, or who have a son
and wanted a girl-bride to raise

and marry when she gets older.
Or Japanese women walk alone
to the gate, selling themselves

to become the wives of Chinese men.
Auntie clucks her tongue
in disapproval. "I will never do

that to the two of you, you hear,
Natsu, I will never sell you two
just so that I can live."

But I hear mothers crying
inside the toilet stalls,
pressing their mouths against

their hands so that the only thing you hear
is the choking sound
as if they are having a heart attack.

Wintering City

The snow has turned the streets white.
There is no one working on the street.

The only thing I can do is to stay inside
in our broom closet. Asa and I huddle

close to each other, and I hope
that we can wake up in the morning

alive, and that spring comes
sooner than never.

RUMORS

People say that all the men
who survived the Soviet invasion
were taken up north across

the Soviet border to a place called
Gulag where they make the men
work sixteen hours a day

in the coldest place on Earth.
People say that the Americans
wiped Japan, no one is alive,

and that's why there is no boat
that can take us back to Japan.
Because nothing is left.

Even the Emperor has been killed.
People say that Japan is now a part
of America, and just like

the black people who were slaves
a hundred years ago in America,
Japanese are now slaves.

People say that Japan was
run over by the Soviets
just like Manchuria,

and what happened
in Saipan and Guam
and in Manchuria

happened in Japan, where people killed
themselves rather than surrender
and live the life of shame.

I don't trust anything
anyone says.
It's like on that day

I found out about
Japan's surrender.
All the things I thought

were true were lies,
and only lies matter
in this world now.

THE BATH

Asa and I take off
our shirts, flapping them

like surrendering enemies
flapping white flags,

shaking the shirts against the fire.
Lice eggs fall out,

pop against the open fire.
Asa stands there

without her shirt,
ribs sticking out

like fishbones in her chest.
Asa points at my chest,

"Natsu-chan, you have *breasts*!"
and laughs. My face burns.

I punch her arm,
and she giggles.

I shake the shirt again,
and more white eggs pop into the fire.

We laugh as we watch
lice pop to death.

At least they died warm,
at least they died without knowing.

Emptying Classrooms

People are no longer arriving.
They are disappearing.

One day the entire classroom
is emptied out.

The next day there are more
naked bodies in the hole.

Sometimes, it is the children
who are herded out

like ducks about to be slaughtered
by the men from the Japanese

community center.
They're taken to an orphanage

somewhere outside
the city. Sometimes

they just disappear
and nobody sees them

ever again.
Just like cats do

when they know they are
about to die.

RUMORS OF GOING HOME

The word about the boat taking us
back to Japan starts from the Teachers'
room to the First Year's Classroom
to the Second Year's Classroom

through the library to the third floor
and the Third Year's Classroom
then to where we are in the closet.
Next day, different news: there is no

boat taking us back to Japan.
But instead, the Soviets are rounding
us up and taking us across the border
to the gulags, where they treat

people like slaves and even slaves are better
off than being with the Soviets, I think.
Men from the Japanese Community,
men who are go-betweens with us

and Russians, us and Chinese,
make sure everyone is looked after.
They go around asking what we need,
they tell us which rumors are lies

and which rumors may be correct. A week later,
there is news that a school is starting up,
and this rumor turns out to be true,
though how I wish it was a lie.

SCHOOL

I tell Auntie I don't want to
go to school. There's nothing
I need to learn. I need to look

after Asa, doesn't she know? Auntie peels off
my jacket heavy with dirt and grime,
my sweater I haven't taken off

ever since August, my shirt that is gray
and she takes a wet sponge,
rubs my body head to toe,

then roughly rubs my shorn head
to shake off the lice.
My body's covered in goose bumps.

She hands me a clean shirt,
a sweater and jacket
that must have come from . . .

and I shake that thought away.
She's not done.
"You go to school in these clothes,

you hear, you go to school
and come back and tell me
what's going on in the world."

I smell of soap. I smell of Auntie.
I smell of something close to home
for the first time since forever.

Learning and Forgetting

For the first time in so many months,
I sit in a classroom not to live
but to learn. There is a teacher,
Miss Tanaka. There are twenty or so

sixth graders just like me.
There is no bowing to the Emperor
like we used to do.
There is no combat training.

And there is no book we read out of.
The blackboard is covered with messages,
messages from people who are looking
for their families, *Misako Shinoda was here*

but moved on to the Manchurian Film Production building;
Mother and Shizuko dead, I'm looking for you, Father.
Miss Tanaka says that there is no textbook,
there is no paper, there is no chalk,

so instead, she recites a passage
from *The Tale of Genji*, and we repeat
it, word for word, line by line.
And my heart feels light for the first time

in so many months, and I forget
about everything, my hunger, my life
in the closet, Asa, Auntie, what I've been
through. Even Tochan.

DEAD DOESN'T NEED IT ANYMORE

A little girl lies atop the pile
of bodies still wearing
her coat and shoes.

(I look and I don't feel anything.)

A dead little girl lies
fully clothed amid
the dead, her eyes closed.
She looks almost asleep.

(I look and I don't feel anything.)

I go down the steep ditch.
I stand atop the dead bodies.

(I look and I don't feel anything.)

I pull off the shoes from her stiff feet.
I take off her socks.
I take her coat off, and her sweater as well.

(I see and I don't feel anything.)

Asa needs shoes.
The dead girl doesn't.

(I do this, and I don't feel anything.
What is happening to me?)

A New Year

Instead of sorghum gruel,
we each get two pieces
of toasted sticky rice.
When I ask

what's the occasion,
the Japanese Community men say
that it's New Year's Day.
I take a bite out of one piece,

and it tastes almost like home.
But not quite.
"Happy New Year,"
Asa says seriously

as she bows deeply,
just like we used to back home.
"Happy New Year, Natsu,"
Auntie says, "sorry I can't give

you New Year's money,
but I can give you some fleas."
And she laughs. Asa laughs.
And like all laughter, it catches

me, and lightness bubbles up
from my stomach to my nose
and I can't keep it in:
I laugh and laugh

until tears fall from my eyes.
And I keep laughing still.

SEEING

Today, I saw, in front of me,
Tochan, his back bent, his hair long,
wearing the khaki of the army, walking

away. I pushed an old woman in a fur.
I pushed people aside and they cursed at me.
But I didn't care. "Tochan, Tochan!"

I yelled but he kept walking away. So I ran
after him. I pushed people out of the way,
and finally reached him. I grabbed his arm, "Tochan,"

but when he turned around,
he looked at me strangely.
It wasn't my father. I apologized,

the words freezing into white breath
with each and every syllable.
I kept saying that under my breath, apologizing

until I got back to the school.
I pushed away the Chinese
people looking for brides and children

to adopt, pinching hard
the hand that grabbed
my arm wanting me, and I ran into the closet

and into Auntie's arms and she asked
what was wrong, and I said,
"I thought I saw Tochan."

And without saying a word,
she pulled me close to her
and pressed me against her chest

and something broke inside of me.
And I cried and cried and cried
and she coughed with each of my sobs.

The Quiet Ground

The snow falls quietly,
again covering the whole

land into an empty space.
Underneath this emptiness

there are mothers,
daughters, sons, and sometimes no

one special because they died alone,
waiting for spring to thaw

the winter away, so they can be
properly buried to go to the other world.

But if I look closely enough,
I see a foot or a hand sticking out

like a shoot of a plant
in early spring.

PART SIX

DEPTH OF WINTER

THE PAST IS GONE

I still think of the bright red sunset
that bursts out on the horizon
then sinks slowly as the night comes.

I still think of the smell of the hay,
the smell of Horse's mane,
and how her heart would beat fast

between my legs as I rode her.
I still think of the chickens that were frightened
of me whenever I kicked them

when I was angry, and how perfect
their warm eggs were in my hands.
I still think of Tochan's laugh

and his strong arms lifting the handles
of the wheelbarrow full of cabbages
and carrots and potatoes.

I still think of our life back north
where we woke up with the sun,
where we slept with the moon,

where things were simple
and we were happy.
Our old neighbors have scattered

to this or that refugee camp,
and our new neighbors are strangers.
But what matters is today,

not the past, never the past.
I can't think of the past
if I want us to stay alive today.

THE CHINESE NEW YEAR

The city turns bright red like the horizon up north
in ghost-Manchuria except that it's the lanterns
and posters and cloths the color of blood,

the color of the Soviet flag, red and as bright as the sun
of the former Japanese flag. The dragons snake around
the streets followed by bangs and gongs of steel drums,

the firecrackers going off like bombs here and there,
never-ending until late at night. And with the pops and cracks
the soldiers shoot their rifles into the air drunkenly,

and we cower, knowing that soldiers do things when they've
had too much to drink and they feel too happy
to care about the freezing temperature.

We stand in the alley, Auntie, Asa, and I,
bundled up in our best rags. Auntie coughs. Asa just leans
closer to me without saying a word, her body so light

next to mine she seems almost a ghost sitting next to the living.
A happy new year? A lit firecracker lands by our feet.
I kick it into the crowd. A happy new year? Not for us.

ALMOST SPRING

Auntie spends most of the day
curled up, coughing weakly,
holding her mouth against

the thinned sleeve of her coat,
trying to be quiet.
Her body shakes, racks,

as if she is the cough itself.
She shakes, she trembles,
she shivers. She is hot

to my touch. Auntie does not
say anything; instead, she curls up
on her side, bearing it all down.

She is getting smaller,
though she is still tough
as Horse's teeth,

but even her stubbornness
seems to be becoming
soft as newly fallen snow.

She pushes Asa away
when she lies next to her.
"You'll catch what I have."

Miss Tanaka, my teacher, stops by,
worried about me being absent,
and then becomes even more worried about Auntie,

but the rest of the time, it's as if
everyone is afraid of her. The only thing
I can do is to give her my half

of the gruel, and rub her back
again and again when she coughs
like the thunder in the prairie up north.

I rub and rub in a prayer,
"Please get well soon.
Please get well soon, Auntie."

I don't say, *You're my family.*
You're like the grandmother
I never had. I love you.

ALL IS NOT WELL

Asa comes back with a bowl
of water from the well,
her hands red from the cold.
I lift Auntie's head and pour

some water down her throat.
She coughs, and it comes trickling
out like a broken well pump,
a little at a time.

Asa wipes Auntie's mouth
with her sleeve.
We get out of the closet
so that Auntie can rest.

Asa looks at the bowl
and suddenly asks me,
"Is Auntie going to be like Kachan?"
Words are caught in my throat.

LIGHT AS A SMALL CHICK

Auntie weighs nothing
when I pull her up
so she can change

position. She keeps
her eyes closed
when I try to feed her.

"Open your mouth, Auntie,
you have to eat," I tell her,
and in response she opens

her mouth like a small chick
that was hatched out
of the egg only a minute ago.

I push in a spoonful,
and she takes half a sip,
then coughs, her small body

trembling and shaking.
I press a broken-off icicle
against her forehead.

My eyes sting, but I push away
the tears. I can't cry right now.
I need to be brave.

I'm the only one
who can take care
of Auntie and Asa.

There Is Nothing I Can Do

I take Kachan's ring and her gold fillings
from the bottom of the pack and hold
them in my hand. They sit cold

like hailstones in late spring.
Asa and I look at them.
"Tochan told me never to use them

but it's an emergency," I say,
and Asa nods, "This is an emergency."
I leave Asa to look after Auntie;

I tell her I will be back. I put on a jacket
Auntie gave me for school. A hat
and pants she made out of burlap sacks.

I put Auntie's shawl around my face.
I am ready. I go out of the school,
pushing away the Chinese

people chanting, "Sell us your children"
to the doctor's clinic five blocks down
through sheets and sheets of blizzard

to knock on his door. I tell him
I require his service, that my auntie is sick,
and he puts his coat on and follows me home.

The doctor holds Auntie's wrist
and closes his eyes, feeling the pulse
of her life. He takes out a stethoscope

and listens to Auntie's heart.
He tells her to cough, and she coughs,
then she can't stop. He asks me

about my mother. I tell him
she's dead. I tell him Auntie is my family,
she's all the family we've got.

After we leave the closet, he looks
at me for a long time. He looks
at me like he is weighing me. I look back at him

without looking down. He looks like
he's about to laugh or cry, I'm not sure.
"Your auntie's very tired. She needs rest,

she needs food, she needs to be
somewhere warm and needs
a hot bath," he says very slowly.

And I tell him, "I got gold. I got
money. Tell me what I have to do,"
and I show him Kachan's gold ring

and gold fillings. "Take it. Make Auntie
better." He shakes his head. "I don't
want your money . . ." and he asks

for my name. "Natsu, I don't
want your money. But I have no
medicine. I have no food. I can't

do anything for your auntie."
My eyes sting, I throw the gold
at him, "I have gold. Make her better.

You're a doctor. That's your job!"
He shakes his head. "I'm so sorry.
There's nothing I can do."

Making Her Stay

I press my body against Auntie's curled-
up one. I curl up just like we used to

when we first arrived here, and we curled
up against one another to keep one another

warm, except this time around, I want
to take away her fever, so she can be better.

"Natsu, don't get close to me," Auntie coughs.
"I don't want you to get sick."

I don't care. I don't care about anything.
"You have to stay healthy for Asa.

If something happens to you, how is she
going to keep going on her own?"

I don't care. I don't care about anything
except for Auntie. "Listen to me, Natsu,"

she slowly turns around, gasping each time
she adjusts her body, "Listen to me,"

she faces me, "You lose when you die,
do you understand? You lose when you die,

so you have to keep living. No matter what."
I press my face into her chest. She puts

her arm around my body.
I put my arm tighter around her

but she feels like she's about to float away,
so light, so small she is. "I don't want you

to go," I whisper into her.
Auntie's hand presses hard against my back.

"I promised your father I'd look after you two,
but I don't think I can keep that promise.

Natsu, promise me this: you'll remember
that no matter what, no matter what happens,

you have to stay alive, do you hear? For Asa." The only thing
I can do is nod to keep the wail that's about

to erupt like a volcano from coming out.
I will hold her as long as I need to,

only if she will not fly away like Kachan did.
I will hold her down here with me and Asa

as long as she can
stay here with us.

PRAYERS

I pray to Kachan.
I pray to Goat.

I pray to Buddha.
I even pray to the Emperor,

Make Auntie get better.
Make Auntie well.

I promise I'll do anything.
You can take my life

if you just let Auntie
get better. No one

answers as Auntie gets
worse and worse,

her fever never coming
down, her eyes becoming

more and more unfocused.
Don't go, Auntie, please.

No. I can't. Keep going.
If I. Lose you.

AUNTIE

I smooth down Auntie's white hair.
Asa takes a rag and cleans Auntie's face.
I take out a photo of Auntie's family,
Taro and Auntie's husband and her—

and open Auntie's clawlike hands, one finger
at a time, and place the photo there.
Asa draws a picture of the two of us
on an old newspaper

and puts it in Auntie's pants pocket.
We fold her body into the sheet
we bought with Kachan's ring and gold fillings
and sew her in with her needle so she won't have to lie

in the hole, freezing even in the other world.
We follow the men from the Japanese Community
carrying Auntie's body out of our closet
through the hallway, where people look away

as soon as they see that someone has died,
as if death is contagious and just acknowledging it
would kill them immediately; we follow
them out of the door into the freezing yard.

And they swing her body, once, twice,
then throw her into the hole.
Her body falls atop the others.
The men put their hands together and pray quickly.

We wait until they are gone
before we throw snow atop her body
so no one will try to steal her clothing,
so that she will be hidden under the snow,

so that she will be able to rest at peace.
I killed her because my love for her
was strong enough to keep us here.
Just like Kachan, she died and left us all alone.

The Empty Space

The space between Asa and me,
where Auntie used to sleep
with her arms around us,

is empty. I clutch her worn backpack
as close as I can to keep it
for when she comes back,

though she's never coming back.
I keep it next to me so I can keep
smelling her. And when I need

to cry, I can bury my face
into the pack without Asa
hearing me. The broom closet feels

so vast without her,
without her big and fearless love.
There is no river anymore.

There is Asa. There is me.
And a big space where
Auntie should be.

THERE IS NO END TO GRIEVING

In the morning,
I turn to Auntie

and find that she is
not there.

In the afternoon,
when Asa and I come

back from school,
the closet is empty

except for our stuff.
And at night,

when I want to tell her
about my day,

there is no one
but Asa.

The Weight of Auntie and Tochan

"Maybe you shouldn't be here,"
Miss Tanaka says as soon as she sees

me standing by the doorway.
Other kids turn around to watch,

but they look away as if they know,
like they know what has happened,

and what I'm feeling. I don't say
anything as I walk slowly

between my classmates sitting
on the floor, and sit next to Sadako-chan.

"Sorry to hear about your auntie,"
she whispers. "My grandma died, too."

The class starts. Miss Tanaka is reading
something but words enter one ear

and leave out the other.
Auntie's bag and Tochan's bag

sit on my lap like stones. Like rocks.
Minutes feel like weeks, and weeks

feel like years, and soon enough
the class is over and Sadako-chan whispers,

"I'm so sorry about your auntie,"
and runs out of the room—she always has

to go back to the cafeteria
where she and her family live

to look after her little brothers.
Miss Tanaka comes over and kneels

down, our eyes at the same level.
"If there's anything I can do,

please let me know," she says kindly.
I look away. I hoist Auntie's bag on my

right shoulder, and Tochan's bag on my left
and walk away from her.

THE NEWSREEL

Miss Tanaka walks ahead of us,
and the Sixth Year follows her
through the hallway

where we meet the First Year.
Asa waves at me and I wave back.
Then the Fifth Year joins us

and we reach the gym
where we are told to sit
on the floor. The curtains

are pulled; the gym becomes dark.
And suddenly, a bright rectangle
appears in front of us

and there, in front of me, are English words
and the picture of a flattened city
and people going about the streets

and American GIs on jeeps
and the Emperor walking around in his suit
and kids like us sitting in front of a shack

eating something steaming from a bowl
and it all stops. No one says a word.
"That is the news from Japan," a man tells us.

A PROMISE

Asa, listen to me.
Take your thumb out.

This is serious.
Don't ever tell

any of the adults that Auntie died.
You know what they do

when kids don't have
their pa's and ma's?

They take the kids away
and they put them

in a really bad place
called orphanage,

and separate brothers and sisters.
I heard that sometimes

they are given away
to the Chinese.

If that happens to us,
they'll separate us,

and we'll never see each
other ever again.

I mean it. If men from the Japanese
Community come, hide. If they tell

you to come with them,
run as fast as you can.

You can't trust anyone here.
I'm serious, Asa.

We have to stick together,
you hear? It's not a game anymore.

WALKING THE STREETS OF HARBIN

Asa and I walk through the narrow labyrinthine
streets, past the onion-shaped dome and the brick-layered

houses, past the fur-clad people and Japanese men begging.
Asa stops: "Look," and points at an old man exhaling rings

from a pipe, his thin beard so long it touches
the cobblestone street. He wrinkles his face and gives us

a toothless smile. A yellow dog scampers past us
with her tail between the legs, followed by a cat going

about her business, whatever her business is.
And for a minute, I almost think it is spring.

But winter has dug in its heels: back in our closet room,
the floor is so cold that no matter how many layers

I wear, the cold seeps through the cloth
and claws its way toward the center of my bones.

SOMETHING DOESN'T FEEL RIGHT

My joints ache
like I had gotten
in a fight the day before
and someone kicked
me real good.
My head feels
heavy, like I'm carrying
a basket of rocks.
My body feels
cold one minute,
as if someone
poured frozen water
over me, I can't get warm.
And the next minute,
I'm burning like someone
is roasting me alive.
What is happening?

So Much Pain

I wake up in pain I wake up with pain in my stomach the bucket in the closet is already full from all that I've thrown up I wake up Asa I really have to go to the bathroom but I'm scared to go by myself but I don't tell her that I tell her I always go with you I whisper as I shake her awake and Asa mumbles something and tells me to use the bathroom in the hallway No way, I'd have to clean it, and the ice chippings get all over my clothes I whisper urgently as my stomach cramps again, hard Natsu-chan, I'm really sleepy she mumbles but she slowly gets up and we hold hands as we walk through the hallway lit only by the moonlight, through the frozen piles of waste and through the light chorus of snores behind the doors and then we move outside into the yard, Asa's fingers tracing along the brick walls, her sleeve pulled over her hand and I hold my hand over my stomach It's so cold and her breath comes out white, and her hand shakes inside mine and she asks me Are you going to make it I'll try I answer and concentrate on holding everything in as another pain hits me and Asa says We're almost there; try not to go in your pants she says loudly as she tugs my hand toward the latrine a ditch with boards laid across it like small bridges the smell acidic and putrid even frozen dizzying us and I have no time to worry about the smell—I pull down my pants as quickly as I can as I stand astride the hole Try not to fall—the ground's completely frozen you could fall in Asa whispers but I feel so bad and my knees are shaking and I feel like I'm floating in air Hurry I'm freezing Asa whispers loudly and I just grunt and let the liquid squirt out of me, liquid that seems never to stop freezing from the moment that it comes out and when it lands in the bottom it thumps against the bottom of the ditch and I feel so sick and I don't know what to do and I've seen so many deaths to know that I am sick and I am like Auntie and I'm going to die just like all the dead lying in the hole waiting for spring to come

FRAGMENTED THOUGHTS

    Asa is going to die
         if she stays with me.
              I've seen too many people

die to know I am going to die, just like Auntie

Who's going to take care of her if—when?—
I die. I don't want to die. I can't die.

        I promised Tochan
            I would take Asa back
to Japan. I promised Auntie.
    If something happens to me, what's going to happen to Asa?
         I don't want Asa
             to die. If I take her
to a Chinese family,
      she will be adopted.
          She will be their daughter.
          Asa's too young to take
          care of herself.

      I want Asa
            to live. I want Asa
to live.
      I am dying.
I don't want to die. But I've seen too many people die, and I know
I'm dying.

Auntie's Ghost

You lose when you die, so you have to keep living.

Where did I hear that?
> *You lose when you die, so you have to keep living.*

Who said that to me?
You lose when you die, so you have to keep living.

I open my eyes
> and I see Auntie standing
>> close to me.

You lose when you die,
> she seems to whisper.

LOVE

Each time I breathe
        a column of white plume
                comes out. The night is

long, the minutes weigh
        as heavy as thick icicles.
                I am awake. I am asleep.

I don't know what to do.
        I know what I have to do.
                I put my arms around Asa

and squeeze her hard.
        I don't know what I should do.
                What would Auntie tell me,

if she were here? What would
        Tochan say? Then I know:
                when I die, who is going to take

care of her. Before I die,
        I have to make sure
                she will be okay after I die.

AN APOLOGY

Tochan, I can't keep
your promise.
I'm so so sorry.
I'm sorry
I can't keep
your promise.

THE MORNING

The morning is about
        to break the dark apart.

I hear the honking of cars
        and trams making

their first rounds of
        picking up people going

to work. I hear
        people beginning

to stir in rooms
        near the closet.

I watch Asa's face,
        and I touch her cheeks

again and again.
        I love you. I love you.

I'm doing this
        because I want you to be taken

care of after I die. I want Asa to live.
        I hear people doing

what they always do:
        washing faces, waking

up, opening their doors,
        eating breakfast.

I push myself out of the closet
        but the floor feels watery.

I take a step, then another.
        I will find a new home for her.

SLEEPING ASA

I find the kindest pair
>   of eyes in the crowd

standing outside of the gate
>   calling out for Japanese children,

a green pair of eyes
>   that belong to an old Russian

woman. She is in furs,
>   and she looks rich.

As if she's been waiting for *me*.
>   she stands there, away

from people as if she knew
>   I would be here.

I take her inside.
>   I show her sleeping Asa.

I show that she is asleep.
>   That she is pretty and cute.

The Russian woman smiles.
>   She tells her Chinese servant to pick

up Asa. She asks, "What about
>   you? Come with me."

I shake my head. She tells me
          thank you. She gives me

a piece of paper with her address
          and some money.

She takes the sleeping Asa away.
          A weight has been lifted

off me—she is going to be okay
          after I die. I have just pulled

my heart out, and I am left with the bloody
          heart beating in my hand.

I WANT TO GO

My lungs hurt and I can't think straight
and all my joints are lit with fire. I see Tochan walking

      through the door and he tells me that
he wants milk, and Goat jumps happily on the frozen ground

           (my head feels like someone's hammering my skull from
                the inside out)
and I want milk, and I want berries, and Horse wants sugar.

                (I can't make it to the bathroom)
and Kachan walks in with Asa (and I'm so cold) and they say

that they are taking me back home. And I say that I don't want—
           (I throw up) I say I don't want to go with them.

           I have to get Asa but Auntie tells me (I'm burning up, I'm
                burning up)
that I don't need to go but I want to go because I have no more
     heart left,

and what am I supposed to do without a heart for the rest of my life?

TOCHAN, KACHAN, AND SNOW

Tochan reaches over and touches
                    my cheek. His hand is as cold
          as ice, like the northern plain,
like the frozen well.
                              He says that I am strong,
          that I have been like a good *chonan*,
looking after Asa,
                    and that Kachan and he are doing good.
Now, Natsu, give me your backpack,
          I can carry it for you,
and I clutch the backpack close to me. I push
          his hand away.
You are a liar. You're not with Kachan,
          you can't have died. He smiles
                    and says nothing as he fades away
          like the dying of the blizzard,
until there is only a swirl
          of outline left, then gone,
                    like he was never here.

SLOW THUDDING OF MY HEART

The days seem to float
        away, sometimes standing

still, sometimes moving
        fast. My body feels heavy,

as if I were a butterfly
        pinned as a specimen

and someone pulls my arm,
        they press cold metals

against my chest,
        and I tell them to stop

but my mouth is frozen shut
        and my body is pinned

to the floor. I want to stay here,
        only if I don't have to feel

the slow thudding of my heart
        beating, beating, closer to death.

THIS IS DEATH

If this is dying,
                    I am happy to die.
          I am glad
I can die before
                    Asa.
          I am glad
Asa is with someone
                    who can take care of her.
          I am glad
she doesn't have to watch me die.
          If this is dying,
     I am ready
          to go.

PART SEVEN

END OF WINTER

COMING BACK TO LIFE

When I come to, someone is holding
my hand. She tells me that I got very sick,

and for a while, no one thought I would
come back. But I did. And she says

that the doctor thinks I am over the worst.
I shake my head. I look around.

I am in a strange room, not in my closet.
And I remember: Auntie died.

I got sick. I gave up Asa.
And I remember: I sold Asa.

No matter how I look at it,
I have given away my own sister.

MISS TANAKA

I go through my pack. The woman tells me
that I held on to it even when I was dying,

but she made sure no one went near it. She says
her name is Tanaka, and she is my teacher.

I look closely at her. I don't remember her.
Then I do: yes, she is Miss Tanaka.

"When you didn't show up to school
for three days, I got worried. I knew you were

with your sister—with your guardian dead.
I'm glad I showed up when I did, I found you

unconscious and dying," she says and presses her hand
against my forehead. I turn away from her.

She doesn't know what I am feeling.
She doesn't know I killed Auntie.

She doesn't know I sold Asa.
She doesn't know. And I can't tell her.

Don't trust anyone here, Natsu.
My heart feels like someone is squeezing it.

"I wish you had told me what was going on,
I could have helped you," she looks straight at me.

"You're staying with me until you are better,"
and she puts her hand on my cheek,

"and once you get better, you can worry about your sister." And I remember:

I have the address. I can go see if the Russian woman will give me back my Asa.

SPRING COMES WITH THE YELLOW WIND AND MAO

The Soviets packed up winter
in the pockets of their uniforms
and they rolled up kilometers
of snow into their backpacks.

They broke off the icicles
and threw them onto
the backs of their trucks
and drove off northward.

And with spring comes Mao's soldiers
with the yellow wind from Mongolia,
walking like cats, their steps not in step,
this man walking this way, that man walking

as if he's carrying a hoe on his back
instead of a rifle, his pants with patches
and holes. The Chinese people come
out waving their hands.

From the yellow flag with the red, blue, white,
and black of Manchuria, to show five races
in harmony, to the flag of the Rising Sun,
to the hammer and sickle, Harbin has

gone through four flags in one year.
Every time the flag changes,
Chinese people come out to celebrate.
Even the branches on the trees

are turning pale green,
and from the window, I can see
people shedding one layer at a time
as each day progresses.

I feel alone like I never have felt before.

THE RIVER OF TIME

Days seem to move fast. Slow.
I can't tell. I close my eyes
and I am awake, and it is

a week later, or a few days later,
I don't know. Nothing stays
the same. Time doesn't stand

still. But there is always
Miss Tanaka, when she is not
teaching, by my bedside.

SPRING BURIALS

Men go down the hole
in the yard and throw
the bodies, one after another,
out of their wintry graves.

Before the bodies thaw
fully, they pull them out
like they would
potatoes, and throw

them into the back
of the truck to cremate.
I watch a bundle of white sheet
being pulled up from the hole.

I know that's Auntie.
I put my hands together
and pray that she is happier
where she is.

Families watch
with their hands pressed
together in the form
of prayer, praying

that their loved ones
can go to the other world
finally now that
spring is here.

THE RED DOOR

I sit on the steps in front
of the red door, the address
that the Russian woman gave
me when I sold my sister.

Maybe Asa is happier.
Maybe Asa has forgotten
about me already.
Maybe she's angry.

Maybe she's dead.
That's when the red door bursts open
and I see the old Russian woman coming
out of the house. I hear the pattering

of footsteps from the interior
of the house, and then Asa
—her face rounder and with pink cheeks
just like back home so many months ago—

pokes her head out. I hold my breath.
It is Asa, just as she was.
And looking healthy.
Then the door closes

before I have a chance to speak.
But my heart bursts.
My steps feel light. I walk
on clouds, as if I've been

pulled to the sky.
Asa's safe, my heart sings.
Asa's safe. She's all right.
My heart sings and sings.

THE OFFICIAL NEWS

It is official.
We are to begin
moving out

of the school
and there will be
a boat to take us

to Japan,
our "repatriation"
back to Japan soon.

But I'm not leaving.
I'm not leaving
until I have Asa,

until it's me and Asa
going back to Japan,
just like I promised Tochan.

UNTIL THE DAY I DIE

I wake up in the morning.
I know what I have to do.
I leave without telling Miss Tanaka

where I am going.
I walk through the busy boulevard
with trees already dark

green and summery,
but I don't stop. I keep walking
until I get to the house

with the red door and I knock.
The servant opens the door.
I tell him I want to talk

to the Russian lady here,
and he tries to stop me,
but I walk in, not bothering

to take off my shoes,
not bothering to be polite.
I walk straight through

the hallway and into the living
room, or so I think,
where I find an old Russian woman

sitting on a velvet couch
with Asa next to her.
"Natsu-chan!" Asa yells,

running toward me, but the woman
pulls her back. "Natsu-chan, I knew it,
I knew you'd be alive! I knew

you'd come get me!" Asa wriggles
in the woman's arms, she bites,
kicks, but the woman ignores it all.

"I came to get my sister back,"
I demand, my heart beating
fast, faster, bravely,

though my mouth is as dry
as the ground in drought.
"She's my child now,"

the Russian woman says
in broken Chinese,
enough for me to understand,

and puts her arm
around Asa.
Asa wriggles away.

"I paid you already.
She's my daughter now," she says.
She looks up and down, at me,

and adds, "You can't provide
the life she deserves."
"She's my sister," I yell,

my hand curling into a tight
fist. "I have your money, take it,"
and I throw the money at her.

"You have to leave now," she says,
dismissing me, and the old servant looks
at me as if to say, "Go, please go."

I lunge at Asa, try to pull her to me,
and the servant lifts me under his arm
and carries me down the hall.

"Asa! Asa!" I yell out her name,
trying to hold on to anything,
everything, but my hands slip.

"I'm coming back every day
until you return Asa to me,"
I yell as I am thrown out of the house

and lie on the dirty stone-
paved street. I promise. I will
make their life a living hell

until I can get Asa back.

TENTH DAY

It's been ten days,
and I've come to the red door

and sat at their steps
every day.

Whenever somebody
walked by, I would chant,

"They stole my sister.
They stole my sister

and I am here to reclaim her."
People gave me funny looks

the first week but now
they smile or give me food.

The old servant comes out once
in a while and brings

a cup of tea or some food.
"I'm not supposed to talk to you,

but you looked hungry
so I brought you some leftovers.

She's a good woman.
She really took care

of your little sister when she first
came here. Your sister was so

difficult, demanding that we take
her back to you, and we had to tell

her that you were dead. Why did you
show up when she finally settled? Just forget

about your sister," he tells me kindly,
and goes back inside.

She may be stubborn
but I am more stubborn.

"They stole my sister.
They stole my sister

and I am here to reclaim her,"
I chant, my throat drying up.

But I keep chanting, chanting,
to get Asa out of the house

and back to where she belongs: with me.
A man walks by and I chant,

"They stole my sister,"
pointing at the red door.

The man smiles and pats my head.
A Chinese servant walks

by with a basket full
of tofu and green leaves.

"They stole my sister,"
I say and she looks away.

The Russian woman pokes
her head out of the door.

"I'm not giving her back,"
she yells, and I yell back,

"You stole my sister.
You're a thief, old lady!"

She slams the door shut.
I'll wear down her stubbornness

with my own stubbornness
like a stone losing its edges

in the strong river current
over many years.

DISAPPEARING CHINESE

The gate of a mansion burst
open, and a man in a long silk robe
came out, his hands tied

in the back. The Communist
soldiers yelled something
about how he was a capitalist

and a collaborator of Imperialist
Japan. The last I saw, he was
being led away from the mansion

with his family huddling
in the corner, crying out his name.
Like the Japanese men

disappearing when the Russians
came to the city.
I close my eyes and keep walking.

THREE MORE WEEKS

Miss Tanaka says that
we will leave
the schoolroom

in mid-July,
three weeks
from now.

I only have
three weeks
to get Asa back.

RAIN

Raining today. People walk by
with umbrellas, not paying attention
to me sitting on the steps. My clothes

are heavy, but this is my job.
Like begging back in winter,
like working on the farm,

this is my job now: getting Asa back.
Suddenly, the door opens,
the Russian woman pokes

her head out and yells,
"You're going to catch your death!"
And I yell back, "You stole my sister.

You're a wicked old lady!"
"I paid for her," she yells and slams
the door shut. I stick out my tongue.

The door opens again, and she throws
a yellow umbrella with a pearl handle
at me and slams the door again.

What We Can Take, What We Can't Take

The Japanese Community tells us
that we cannot take any photos,
letters, or notebooks with us;

that we are to take only the necessities:
money up to 1,000 yen,
and whatever clothes still cling

to our shrunken bodies.
Nobody told us why we can't take
these other things.

Maybe they are trying to erase
the history of Manchuria
from our memory,

or from the memory of history itself,
leaving the dead behind in a country
that no longer exists on the map.

A Prayer

Dear Tochan, I know you are not dead
but I hope you can hear me. I got sick.
I got really sick and I thought I was going
to die. And I gave up Asa because I didn't
know what to do if I were to die and she was
left on her own. But I got better. Tochan,
I promise you, I'll get Asa back
and I'll never let her go. So help me this
one time, do something so that the awful
Russian woman will return Asa to me.
Tochan, if you can't hear me,
what about you, Auntie. Can you hear me?
Can you help me get Asa back?
And oh, one more thing, Auntie,
can you tell Tochan to hurry up and come find us?

I Am as Stubborn as Horse

I sit on the steps.
It's a beautiful day,
the temperature not too hot,

not too cold. And if I close
my eyes in these pockets
of moments when no one is on

the street, I can almost imagine
myself back in the settlement,
standing by the gate and looking out

on the never-ending field.
I can almost imagine watching
Tochan leading Horse back

from the field, I can almost hear
other settlers settling in for dinner,
the hamlet busy with a clutter of pots

and plates and of cooked vegetables
with burning soy sauce.
I open my eyes and find myself back

in Harbin, back in front of the red-door
house, and I curse out loud,
"You are a thief, old woman!"

just to remind her I am still here,
that I am not going away until
she returns Asa to me.

SUNDAY

My stomach growls.
There is nothing
to do except to sit

on the steps, waiting
for someone to walk by
so I can chant,

"They stole my sister.
They stole my sister,"
but it's a lazy day.

Maybe it's a day when
the Russians go
to the onion-shaped

dome on the square.
The door opens.
The old servant pokes

his head out, looks around,
and sits next to me, pulling out
a bag of fried doughnuts

sprinkled with sugar.
"I haven't had sugar
in such a long time,"

I wrinkle my nose
in joy and take a bite.
The sweetness spreads

inside of my mouth
and my tongue can't get
enough of it.

"The madam asked about you,"
the old servant says.
"What does she want?"

I ask, then take another big
bite. "She thinks that you are
stubborn, but in a good way."

I am about to take another
bite but I stop. I open my mouth.
"The train leaves

on the third Monday at six a.m.
That's when all the Japanese
have to leave,"

I tell him. He looks down.
The silence between us
heavy but loud

with things I can't hear.
He gets up without a sound.
He closes the door without a word.

WHAT I WILL TAKE WITH ME

I take the photos,
family registry,
birth certificates,

and postal saving books
from my backpack,
and photos and papers

from Auntie's bag,
and sew them into
the lining of my coat,

threading the corners
into the fabric so that they
will not be dislodged.

Auntie's sewing kit
is what I keep because
it's how I remember her: always sewing.

And I will take Auntie's bag
and I will take Asa's hand
and we will both be on the boat.

I've traveled 1,000 *li*
just like the *senninbari* tiger
I gave Tochan,

and I will travel 1,000 *li*
more with Asa until Tochan
will find us wherever we end up.

I sew the pieces
back together to sew
back my past into the present.

THE STUBBORN OLD WOMAN

The red door opens with a bang.
"You, girl, get out of here!"
the Russian woman yells out,

her green eyes turning dark, almost
black, with anger. "You're a thief,
old woman! Give me back my sister!"

I yell at her, shaking my fist.
She waves her cane at me.
We keep waving at each other—

my arm, her cane, until she laughs weakly.
"Here, you must be hungry," and
a bag lands on my lap, a bag full of fried doughnuts.

The Day Before

I bang a rock against the door.
"Give me back my sister.
Give me back my sister,"

I yell with each bang,
and the Russian woman pokes
out her head. "You can do that

all you want, but she's not going
anywhere!" she yells out,
her white hair in its bun

shaking in rhythm with her
raised cane. Then she slams
the door shut and I keep banging

on the door, shouting,
"Give me back my sister.
Give me back my sister,"

even after my voice disappears,
even after the sun sets and the night
has surrounded the neighborhood

and the door doesn't open.

THEN IT DOES

And the Russian woman
comes out holding Asa's hand.
"You won, you stubborn girl.

You take care of your little sister,
you hear? She is a good girl,
and you are a good sister."

And with that, she hugs Asa,
"Don't forget me, little girl,"
and Asa and I are once again one,

our arms around each other,
and I am never letting her go.
My promise to Tochan is fulfilled.

The End

The train keeps moving,
halting, moving, almost
like it's hiccuping through

the landscape so like
the one we walked
to get to Harbin a year ago.

Asa didn't talk to me
for the first hour as we walked
from the Russian woman's house

to the port, but after five thousand
sorrys, she said, "You gave me
away and I was scared.

But Madam Borisovna was nice,
she said that you were really sick
and that you had to send me away

to her until you got better.
She told me later that you might
have died, and she felt bad

that she didn't take you with her.
But I knew you couldn't have died.
I knew you'd come get me.
Here, she gave us a bag of doughnuts."

My arms tighten around Asa
in the crowded cattle train.
Miss Tanaka sits with us,

her bag so small it seems
to fit in her hands.
The train keeps moving,

halting, moving,
southbound, always moving,
and Asa and I hold

each other tight,
and how I wish Auntie was here.
Then we are pushed

into a warehouse
and then onto a ship.
A whistle blows once,

then twice, and the boat slowly
begins to pull out of port.
"Good-bye, good-bye,"

people wave their arms
as hard as they can.
"Good-bye, good-bye,"

I wave my arms,
in the beat of my heart
but my heart is breaking

once, twice, each time I wave:
Auntie. Tochan. Kachan.
Principal Ohara. Toshio's mom.

All the settlers who disappeared.
All the kids who went away
with their new Chinese parents.

Horse. My home back north.
The beautiful prairie and the Wall.
Goat and chickens and our farm.

I keep waving my hand.
Asa squeezes my other hand,
once, twice, a Morse code,

and I squeeze her hand.
Message received and understood.
I look ahead into the vast

wide horizon of the ocean,
like the horizon
of the Manchurian prairie,

so flat, so wide. I am going
somewhere at the end
of the prairie of the sea,

where Tochan will come find us.
The ocean ahead is calm.
The horizon flat. I am ready.

AFTERWORD

Every summer starting in 1975 up until the late 1990s, Japanese-Chinese men and women who were abandoned or left in China right after World War II came to Japan to look for their parents and relatives. Almost all of them looked older than their actual age, and almost all of them didn't speak a word of Japanese.

What they had as proof of their Japanese identity were things that their biological parents—if they were lucky—had left them: clothing and items with their names written on them, perhaps; sometimes, Japanese addresses, but most of the time, they only had pieces of themselves that proved that they were Japanese—their very own names, their parents' names, or just fragments of memories.

Once these Japanese-Chinese got to Japan, there was hope that blood relatives would come to claim them. However, most of the time, these meetings never took place: no one was looking for them because they had already died, or people wanted to forget what had happened right after the war, or because they were declared dead and no one was searching for them.

Where did these Japanese-Chinese men and women come from? I wondered as I watched the television news. *What were Japanese doing in China anyway, and why were they left there?* One summer day, as we watched a new set of now-adult Japanese-Chinese orphans entering the airport arrival area with luggage, craning their necks, searching for possible relatives waiting for them, my mother said—her eyes glued to the television—"Our families never had to go to Manchuria, but I could've been one of them if they had made a different choice." That's when Natsu and her family came to my mind, caught my imagination, and insisted that Natsu's story be written down.

In 1931, the Japanese government overtook the northern part of China and declared it an independent state called Manchukuo with the last emperor of China—Puyi—as the Kangde Emperor of Manchuria. The government of the newly founded Manchuria created a slogan, "Five Races Under One Union," and indeed, there were many races living in the country: the Mongolians, Chinese, Korean, Japanese, Russians (who escaped the Russian Revolution in 1917), and many Europeans. People like Madam Borisovna, a former Russian aristocrat, could live in exile in Harbin because the city was very cosmopolitan.

However, in reality, Manchukuo was a puppet state controlled by the Japanese government.

Japan at that time was suffering from three major issues: overpopulation, bad economy, and lack of natural resources. As a state policy, Japan encouraged its citizens—especially impoverished villages and second and third sons of farmers—to relocate to Manchuria and other occupied territories to provide much needed natural resources for the mainland. With the promise of a better life, men and women, families, uprooted themselves from their homes in Japan to start their lives in the remote areas of the expanding Japanese empire: Saipan, Guam, Taiwan, present-day Korea, Manchuria, Sakhalin Island and four islands north of Hokkaido, and areas that were considered "friendly" to the Japanese: the Philippines, Southeast Asia, parts of China, and the South Pacific islands. Up until 1945, over three million Japanese civilians and nearly the same number of military personnel lived outside of Japan. Natsu's family was among the two million Japanese civilians living in China and Manchuria.

Sometimes the entire village resettled into areas where former Chinese peasants had lived, ignorant of the fact that the land they tilled had just recently been forcibly taken from the Chinese. The settlers had to endure harsh, long winters in less-than-standard huts made out of clay and straw. They were under constant threat from the elements as well as fear of attacks by bandits and Chinese peasants whose lands had been taken away. Settlements farther away from the urban areas oftentimes had to arm themselves, in some cases build walls around their settlements, because they knew that the help was so many days away if they were attacked. Boys between sixteen and nineteen were sent under the Manchurian Youth Pioneers, trained to fight and farm. During 1939 to 1945, military training was part of the school curriculum, both in Manchuria and Japan—both boys and girls were trained to fight at school. For children living in the settlements far away from Japanese Army garrisons, it was not unusual for them to know how to shoot guns as a way of protecting themselves.

The Japanese settlers migrated to these unfamiliar lands out of patriotism, believing that what they were doing was for the good of the nation, and that they were living in harmony with other races. Meanwhile, as World War II thickened and Japan was losing the war from 1942 on, Manchuria remained somewhat unscathed. Propaganda by the Imperial General Headquarters of Japan ensured that the news of Japan losing battles was never made public, so when the Soviet Armed Forces broke into the Manchurian border on August 9, 1945, it came as a surprise to the settlers.

Out of thousands of settlements of various sizes spread over Manchuria, and with most men drafted at the last minute, these settlements were left with elderly men, teenagers, women, and children who had to evacuate to safety without soldiers to protect them. Little did they know that their fathers and sons were left to protect the Manchurian-Soviet border by themselves with only the most basic weapons. They also did not know that the Japanese Imperial Army had already retreated, and with railways unmanned and no accessible automobiles, people had to evacuate by foot. Some villages chose to die as a group when they knew that they could not get away, to die honorably rather than "to live the life of shame," which was taught at school; some were abandoned and left to die on their trek to safety; some, after making it to the major cities where refugee stations were set up, died from malnutrition and below-freezing temperatures. Some parents gave up their children to the Chinese civilians, thinking that with so many people dying of starvation and diseases in refugee camps, they would be saving their lives.

Chinese people, traditionally, put emphasis on keeping the family line going; many childless couples took in orphaned children and raised them as their own. Yeeshan Chan, the author of *Abandoned Japanese in Postwar Manchuria: The Lives of War Orphans and Wives in Two Countries* (2011), pointed out to me, while discussing this manuscript, "The Chinese families that adopted Japanese orphans had faced political punishment. But still, they were willing to take the risk. The infant mortality was very high in Northeast China (Manchuria) during those years. As the demand for adoptive children was very high, there were brokers who bought Japanese orphans and sold them to rural families. It can be concluded, thanks to the market demand for adoptive children, many Japanese children were able to survive in the rural Chinese families." Many of these Japanese orphans raised by their adoptive Chinese parents say that they are grateful for the kindness and bravery of these parents who raised and protected them through this turbulent period of Chinese history: the Civil War between the Nationalists and the Communists, the Great Leap Forward, and the Cultural Revolution.

There are said to be 2,700 recognized Japanese-Chinese children (2013), yet this number does not include children over thirteen years old at the time of the end of war: the Japanese government considers anyone over thirteen who remained in China as having chosen to do so on their own. This 2,700 figure also does not include teenage girls who had no choice but to work as maids in Chinese households or marry themselves off for survival.

Though it is not clear how many people died in total, about 250,000 are said to have lost their lives before they reached Japan in August 1946. Dysentery, which is a curable illness for a healthy person with access to modern medical facilities, claimed many lives, as did starvation and hypothermia; these evacuees, having to live in very unhygienic and cramped situations, who were already undernourished and exhausted, lived in constant fear of illness and death. Those who survived the ordeal did not fare well even when they returned to Japan. Having lost everything—the land, livestock, property, family members, savings—in Manchuria, they had to rebuild their lives from scratch.

Natsu's story is just one of many, and she is one of the luckier ones who came out alive, and somehow made it back to Japan. You may wonder if Tochan ever made it home. Just as in the novel, men were conscripted to the Japanese Imperial Army a couple of weeks before the Surrender on August 15, 1945, from the Manchurian settlements; though the number is contested, about 600,000 Japanese men are said to have been captured by the Soviet Army and sent to gulags in Siberia and former Soviet territories. The working conditions were severe: lack of food plagued them as well as the subzero temperatures, long working hours, poor living situations, and unclean water. Many men died, and those who survived this experience were never the same. One of my uncles, who grew up in Sakhalin (a former Japanese territory, and now part of Russia), was drafted in July of 1945, sent to the Soviet border, and was captured by the

Soviets around August 9, 1945; he was sent to a Siberian gulag, and had to endure five years of manual labor in Kazakhstan as a prisoner of war. He says that he lost so many of his friends there, and it was only through great luck that he survived. He was not yet twenty when he was drafted. I'd like to believe that Tochan came back to Japan and found Natsu and Asa, but the historical facts make me also believe that Tochan, with his kind-heartedness and his sense of rightness, probably did not survive the gulag.

As someone who grew up in three countries (Japan, Belgium, and the US) in the first eight years of my life, having had to learn a new language every time our family moved, being displaced from my home has been a lifelong interest. My story is so different from Natsu's story—because my father worked for a Japanese company, we were protected by the company and the government, unlike Natsu and other settlers in Manchuria (and other territories Japan held until August 1945). Whenever there were battles and wars, his company protocol was—and still is—to evacuate employees and their families as quickly as they can.

When the First Gulf War broke out in 1990, my father was on the team to strategize logistics of evacuating the employees and their families overland if the civilian evacuation flights could not be secured. He told me that he thought of the Manchurian evacuees when he was tasked to come up with the worst-case overland plan: to calculate how long it would take for people to walk from Kuwait City to Saudi Arabia, with only a few able men, no arms to protect them, across a hostile landscape by foot. I still remember him saying, "Do you know how hard it is to tell people that they are on their own until they reach the border, with the Iraqi Army chasing after them?" He said that he was glad his team was able to put the employees and their families on the last civilian plane leaving Kuwait after many uncertain days of waiting at the airport.

This story may feel as if it is a story taking place in the past in a faraway country, but it has repeated many times over—for instance, after the Vietnam War, Vietnamese refugees got on small fishing boats to brave the long journey over treacherous ocean to Thailand or Australia; in the early '90s, Hutu refugees trekked through murderous Rwandan land to reach the neighboring borders of Uganda, Zaire, and other African Great Lakes Region nations; people in Chernobyl had to flee the city they loved because of the nuclear power plant meltdown and were told to pack three days' worth of luggage and food, though the journey turned into decades-long exile; Syrian refugees running away from the military to Turkey and other neighboring countries (2013–present); Japanese people who lived within the twenty-kilometer radius of the Fukushima Daiichi Nuclear Power Plant (2011–present); Rohingyas, the minority Muslim population in Myanmar, fleeing to Bangladesh (2017–present); people making the arduous trek from Central American countries to the southern border of the US, fleeing from unstable and dangerous countries (2014–present). For them, staying home is not an option—leaving home is safer—and it takes so much courage and bravery to leave behind everything you know to reach safety. There are, as of 2018, 65.8 million people who have been driven from home.

Next time you see refugees on the television, put yourself in their shoes: they have left everything they knew and loved to reach a place of safety. Nobody chooses to be a refugee.

The author as a child in Japan

ACKNOWLEDGMENTS

No novel is written in a vacuum. It is a communal effort, though most of the time, the people involved do not know that they are helping a writer as she struggles behind a closed door with the story.

I'd like to thank the nameless woman I met at a temporary housing neighborhood in Fukushima in 2012 when I was doing fieldwork for another book. She sat on her small front step, tending to her flowers. We started talking and she told me that she was a dairy farmer; she told me that when the earthquake and tsunami hit the northeastern coast of Japan on March 11, 2011, her house was too inland to be affected until a few weeks later, when she found out that the radiation plume from the devastated Fukushima Daiichi Nuclear Power Plant had irradiated the cattle feed, and she and her family were ordered to slaughter the affected dairy cows that she had raised like they were her own children. And a few days later, she and her family were forcibly evacuated from the polluted village. She took a deep breath and looked toward the far beautiful mountain ranges of Fukushima, and then whispered, "This isn't the first time I lost my home—I lost my family and my home in Manchuria." She told me about her experience of a harrowing trek across Manchuria with her mother and her siblings, and how she lost her mother and most of her siblings at the refugee camp. By the time she reached Japan, only she and one of her sisters had survived. She was only fifteen years old. As we were saying good-bye, she looked at me and said, "As long as you are alive, you can start all over again." And I saw this elderly woman as she must have looked when she was fifteen years old, and I also saw Natsu, who I had imagined and seen in my dreams for many years, as a real person in this elderly woman.

One big bear hug goes to Jonathan Wu, who is the biggest fan of Asa (who used to be Cricket), who believed in Natsu and this novel from the start, and who kept asking me about Asa and Natsu over dinners—you are the best friend anyone could have.

A very big thank-you to Christy Ottaviano, my wonderful editor and publisher: our relationship started more than twenty years ago, when she hired me as a summer intern as I was trying to figure out what to do, now that I was done with schooling. Her passion for children's literature was infectious—I still have the fever, two decades later. It took me twenty years to learn how to write for children. Thank you for publishing this book, and thank you for teaching me, that summer a long time ago, the beauty and power of children's books.

Also thank you to the following people who have been my road signs on an unmapped journey of writing this book: Yeeshan Chan for thoughtfully reading over the manuscript (I was so relieved when you wrote back to tell me that I got the historical parts right); women and men (who shall remain anonymous here) who shared their stories with me about being *zanryu koji* (Japanese children abandoned in China); and Temple University Japan Campus, my home for the last two decades.

And of course, every book I write is written over many, many conversations with my mother, who is my true north. She may not understand what I do when I disappear to do fieldwork, and she cannot read the books I write—just like Auntie—but she tells me, "Eat, eat," as a way to urge me forward.

ABOUT THE AUTHOR

MARIKO NAGAI is the author *Dust of Eden* and several books of poetry and fiction for adults. She has received the Pushcart Prize in both poetry and fiction, as well as many other accolades. She is an associate professor of creative writing and Japanese literature at Temple University, Japan Campus, in Tokyo, where she is also the director of research. mariko-nagai.com